A Heart Divided

By
Sarah Crandell Thomas

PublishAmerica
Baltimore

First printing

At the specific preference of the author, PublishAmerica allowed this work to remain exactly as the author intended, verbatim, without editorial input.

This is a work of fiction set in a background of history. Public personages both living and dead may appear in the story under their right names. Scenes and dialogue involving them with fictitious characters are of course invented. Any other usage of real people's names is coincidental. Any resemblance of the imaginary characters to actual persons, living or dead, is entirely coincidental.

ISBN: 1-4241-3750-0
PUBLISHED BY PUBLISHAMERICA, LLLP
www.publishamerica.com
Baltimore

Printed in the United States of America

This book is dedicated
to Christian women who live in God's grace
through faith in the Lord Jesus Christ
and who long to dwell in His presence
with clean hands and a pure heart.

Psalms 24:3 & 4
Matt. 5:8

Acknowledgements

When I began to think about acknowledging some of the special people who have been an important part of the development of my first book, I realized that the list could go on and on. I hesitate to name individuals as there is always the concern of inadvertently omitting someone, but I would be remiss not to acknowledge the following people. Please know that regardless of the role you played or whether your name is mentioned here, if you had any part in the creative and prayerful process of writing this book, I thank you from the bottom of my heart.

Thank you, Gwen Crandell Klein, for the love of a big sister and all the support and encouragement you've given me. I appreciate every e-mail and phone call. Thanks, too, for helping with the final edit and helping to bring this project to completion. Now, I look forward to reading your book!

Thank you, Kevin and Michelle Baker who have given so much wise, Godly council and unconditional love beyond measure. May God continue to bless you both.

Thank you, Terese Cossette, for a lifetime of friendship, love, prayers, giggles, and your unconditional support of whatever my latest project was at the time. As kindred spirits, there's a little part of you in so much of what I do; you're never very far away. Wouldn't it be great to just talk it all over a bowl of cream of crab soup with a splash of sherry?

Thank you, my precious Jenny Tritch, for your gift of friendship, constant encouragement, faithful prayers, and limitless enthusiasm. You're always right there, no matter what the need is. You are truly a gift from the Lord, and I am so thankful to have you in my life! Thank you for loving me just as I am.

Thank you dear Mandy Williams for recognizing a dialogue tag when you see one and knowing what to do with it. Thanks for all the help editing, great suggestions, and continual reassurance that "it's *good!*" Thanks especially for your encouragement and boundless joy!

Thanks Erin Weilein for your inspiration, joy, prayers, infectious smile, and love. Can you imagine how boring my life would be without you and your sister?

Thank you, Barb Reinard, for understanding our needs and finding a special home for us. In the midst of writing this book, unexpected job losses initiated our 650-mile move. You quickly moved from our realtor to our friend, and found our tranquil country home that continues to inspire my creativity.

Thank you, Karen Engle for assistance with research and for very capably covering the office so I could meet writing deadlines.

Thank you to the Reynolds family, the Tulsa cousins who shared the gifts of hospitality, encouragement, and some of Mary's priceless treasures.

Finally, I thank you my dear Marty for your patience and understanding of my endless hours at the computer and all the times I said, "I *need* to write!" and disappeared into another world. I so much appreciate that you always give me the freedom, the time, and the space to be creative. This could have been a difficult task without all of your support and your pride in my accomplishments. Thank you for loving me so much.

Introduction

On March 2, 1891, Mary Stevenson Smythe boarded a train in Washington, DC and headed for the American West. She and her traveling companions set out on a three-month journey to see new places and visit old friends and family. She left her husband and home in Maryland, and her daughter. The little girl's grandmother would care for her at the family homestead in New Jersey until Mary returned—or sent—for her daughter. The circumstances surrounding Mary's drastic decision to leave home and family are somewhat vague, but one can surmise from her letters that her marriage to George was a very difficult one.

The letters contained in this book are transcribed from Mary's originals, which are in remarkably excellent condition, and in my possession. Although I have altered most names, I have not otherwise changed the content of the letters themselves. Some sentences run together, some words are misspelled, and some letters end abruptly with no closing. There are initials that I cannot identify, but certainly would be recognized by the recipient of the letter. Mary uses words and expressions typical of her day: 1891. By transcribing nearly as written, it is my desire to share every intimate aspect of Mary's journal. Within the story itself, I have remained factual wherever possible. Where necessary to complete the scene, I have taken liberty.

I have included photographs of some of the people involved in this story. The pictures of Mary, George, Fredericka, Fred, Max, and Aunt Emily are the actual characters and are photos from my family collection. These photographs are not necessarily of the exact time of the writing, but will serve to connect the reader with the main people in this story. I have numerous treasured heirlooms that belonged to Mary, such as the monogram "S" embroidered handkerchief, the fine kid gloves, and the silver spoon that you will read about in this story.

This story reveals one woman's sense of adventure, her inner struggles and her spiritual battles, and American history. It is a reflection of a very different time in our country and in the traditional role of women. Mary ventured outside that tradition, followed the lure to travel and to experience things first-hand, and searched her own heart. She was forced to make decisions with long-term consequences, both for herself and for others. In the end, she was able to reconcile all of the pieces of a heart divided.

The Main Characters

Mary   Mary Stevenson Smythe. My maternal great-grandmother. Born in 1858 in New Orleans, Mary is 32 when this story takes place.

George   George Smythe. Mary's husband and my great-grandfather. Born in 1856 in Mill Creek, Virginia, George, age 35, commutes daily by train between their home in Hyattsville, Maryland and Washington, DC where he works at the main post office.

Aunt Emily Born in 1823, Emily Dennison is Mary's mother's older sister. When Mary's father and sister die suddenly of pneumonia, it is Aunt Emily and her husband, Uncle Isaiah, who would provide a permanent home for the infant Mary and her mother, Sophia. Mary is raised in Newark, NJ along with the Dennison children and is a beloved member of the family. Aunt Emily is 69 years old at the time of this story.

Fredericka Daughter of Mary and George Smythe; my grand mother; my mother's mother. Little Freddie is 16 months old when this story begins, and is staying in Newark, NJ with her Grandmother Sophia, Mary's mother.

Fred   Frederick Dennison is the youngest son of Aunt Emily and Uncle Isaiah Dennison, and Mary's first cousin. Inseparable as children, Fred understands Mary better than anyone else does. Mary and George named their first child after him: Fredericka Dennison Smythe. It is the name 'Fredericka' that my grandmother, mother, and I share. Fred is 31 when this story takes place.

Max   Maxwell Webster is Fred's valet.

Natalie   Mary's sister-in-law; George's unmarried sister. Natalie Smythe frequently lived with her brother and sister-in-law in Maryland.

James   Mary's brother-in-law; George's younger brother. James was still unmarried at this time and would often visit with George and Mary.

Mary Stevenson Smythe
c. *1891*

George M. Smythe
c. 1891

Aunt Emily Dennison
c. 1891

Chapter 1

Monday, March 2, 1891

Her dainty hands were finally warm again, and the flood of tears had just about ebbed as the suburban Maryland countryside passed beyond the window. The early evening light cast an eerie, dim glow on all that was familiar. As the train gained speed, the sway of the car lulled her deeper and deeper into thought. This would be such a wonderful adventure and such a good thing to do. It was *important* to get away. Yes, it was necessary. It was the *right* thing to do, she repeatedly told herself, as if trying to convince no one but herself.

The hot tea with honey was soothing. Chamomile tea was always a comfort, and Aunt Emily always seemed to know just when to have a tray brought in. Even as a little girl when something distressed her, Auntie knew tea would be part of the solution. Silently she wondered if tea would be enough this time, and wondered if she would ever possess the understanding, compassion, and love that both Aunt Emily and Uncle Isaiah exhibited. She was glad Aunt Emily was with her, and that her own mother was not. As dear as she is, it just doesn't always help to have Mother involved in the situation. No, this time it was best that Mother had care of the baby and that Mary have this time without encumbrances.

"Oh, how negligent of me to have misplaced my fine kid gloves," Mary silently and angrily reprimanded herself. "They were absolutely irreplaceable. Certainly, I can acquire more, but these were such a special gift from Uncle Isaiah! It was my twelfth birthday, I believe, or perhaps thirteenth. That seems so very long ago now; so much has happened since that time."

Warm tears once again flooded her eyes and coursed down her porcelain-like cheek.

"There, there dear child. Are you feeling better now?" Aunt Emily's soft voice inquired as she returned and settled her ample self into her seat.

"Yes, thank you," Mary answered softly as she mopped what she certainly hoped would be the very last of her tears.

Opening the tiny silk bag, she stuffed in the soggy handkerchief and took out a freshly pressed one, just in case need be. She drew and tied the delicate pink satin ribbons on the little purse, and gently touched the fine, soft fabric, reflecting that both the bag and the lovely handkerchief, too, were gifts from special people. The dark rose French silk bag was a gift from Fred the very last Christmas that she was home. The elaborately hand-embroidered fine handkerchief was a bridal trousseau gift from Mother. She had had it for years, and it was worn terribly thin. Mary wondered how many tears it had blotted. Certainly, Mother had shed many…Father, Raymond, baby Julia. She examined the remarkably minute stitches of the letter "S", and the delicately fashioned leaves and flowers surrounding the monogram.

"I wonder what we'll find offered on the menu this evening."

"Pardon?" She startled. She was so lost in her own thoughts that even the familiar, gentle voice of Aunt Emily was a jolt.

"Oh! I am so sorry, dear! I won't disturb you further. Supper, dear, I was just babbling on about supper. Unimportant really. I know you want to be quiet and to just be left to yourself for a time. Well, that's fine dear. I know how distressed you are over the loss of your good gloves. I'll hush now, dear. You just try to rest yourself. Perhaps they will be found and turned in. We'll check in with the stationmaster in Chicago at our first opportunity. We'll have him wire Washington to see if they have been turned in. Oh, dear, try not to be fretful! I do hate to see you so sad."

Mary nodded and smiled faintly, but remained silent. She wasn't entirely sure how much of her distress was actually over the loss of those gloves. Precious though they were, she could not help thinking about what the future would hold for her and Mr. Smythe.

Again, her fingers ran over the beautiful "S" on the thin, old handkerchief. "S" for Stevenson her maiden name; "S" for Smythe her wedded name.

"Honestly! I cannot but wonder if any other woman on earth has ever found her husband quite as irksome as I find mine!" Mary's mind screamed to herself. "The very idea of such a public display of that disagreeable disposition of his is most disheartening. It is entirely one matter for Mr. Smythe and me to discuss our differences behind the privacy of the closed doors in our own home, but an entirely different matter for those issues to be taken into public places! I was nearly speechless with that scene, and, may well have been the beneficiary had I remained so."

Another swell of tears spilled over, and, as Mary dabbed at her eyes, Aunt Emily leaned over and gathered Mary's little hands into her own chubby ones.

"Oh, dear, dear," said Aunt Emily as she patted her left hand. "You'll be fine, child, just *fine*. A change will help, and I do think you will feel better once we get a little further on."

Aunt Emily knew these tears were not just about the gloves.

"It's just that George is so...so *very exasperating!*" Mary blurted out, followed by a loud and very unladylike sniffle.

"I know, I know, Mary. However, he is a good man really, and there is no doubt of his love for you. A little time away will do you both good. This time away will give you both a chance to clear those nasty old cobwebs. George will be fine, and you know Fredericka will be very well attended to. They will both be *just fine.*"

Fredericka. Mary's thoughts snapped to her baby girl. Time would prove that she would miss her terribly, and she was already starting to. She was convinced, however, that she needed this time away, regardless of the cost.

Mary would never have entertained the thought of this expedition if not for being able to leave the baby with her Mother. At least Mother consented to that much. Although she strongly disapproved of this little jaunt, she was delighted with the opportunity to have her baby granddaughter with her for an extended time. Mary was surprised that she offered to come to Maryland to pick up the baby rather than having her bring the baby up to Newark. Oh! It was so good to see Mother! They both wished they had more time together. She really is a dear, and really does mean well! She loves Fredericka so, and will be so good with her...

"She will be *fine,*" Aunt Emily repeated as she patted Mary's hand again. "*Just fine,* and so will you."

"Aunt Emily knows me well," Mary thought to herself. "Perhaps she even understands some things that Mother could not. I imagine that Father was all that Mother ever wanted; all that she ever needed. They were so much in love, and had only ever loved each other. I'm sure there was never anyone or anything shy of death that would have ever separated them."

Mary lapsed deep into her thoughts of just how different times were now. Why, certainly many things have changed since her parents wed in 1852.

"This is *1891,* for heaven's sake, and I'm going to see and experience everything I can! I'm a capable woman, and must think for myself! I owe it to myself...and to my daughter of course, to experience all life has to offer! Oh! This trip with Aunt Emily and Fred will be so grand! Why, when Fred joins us...." Her thoughts tried unsuccessfully to capture that moment of reunion.

"Let us freshen up for supper, dear." Again, Aunt Emily's words interrupted Mary's wondering thoughts.

"I can hardly wait to determine for my own self it the fare is nearly half as fine as it is purported to be! Oh! This is such a *lark*! Think of it, Mary: *California!* And once Fred joins us in Hays...." She paused, took a deep breath, and clasped her hands together. "Oh! It will be just so wonderful to see Fred, won't it dear? Just like old times, when we were all together as a family...except with a new adventure! We will see and do so many things! Oh, won't it be *grand*, dear? You'll have so much to write George about!"

Mary returned the beautifully hand-painted teacup to its saucer. Yes, indeed it will be wonderful to see Fred again. That, if anything, was an understatement.

"Yes, I suppose I will have much to tell him," Mary replied.

Silently she wondered if George would even bother to return her correspondence. He was so very angry! She wondered if he would even care that she was away. She wondered how he would spend his time, and she wondered...

"Oh! Enough 'wondering' for now! I have a marvelous adventure ahead of me!" Mary barked silently to herself.

"Yes, Auntie, let's freshen up, then move to the dining car. I think a little supper would be good now," she affirmed.

"Oh, that's wonderful, dear! I'm just so excited! I do hope they have fresh beef! I would love a good cut! And truffle for dessert! Oh, that would be perfectly divine! Just perfectly divine!

Chapter 2

Tuesday, March 3

"Do you realize, Mary dear, what remarkable times we live in?" Aunt Emily launched into conversation as she slathered the fresh, hot biscuit with butter at breakfast the next morning.

"Absolutely *remarkable*" she continued. "Why, who would have ever thought that a person could travel all the way to *California*—by *train!* California, Mary! Think of it! Oh, I could barely sleep last night, for I am just so excited! Such a *healthy* place, I've read. Why, the climate there is unlike any place else in the *world*! Imagine, dear! Flowers bloom there all the year round…but without the humidity of New Orleans, of course."

Aunt Emily cocked her head and lowered her voice. "Wretched place, New Orleans is. Oh, it's fine much of the year, but the humidity in the summer is simply unbearable! I've always been thankful your mother brought you north. Not a proper place at all for a widow and child, that's for certain!"

"Oh, yes, the flowers," she continued without taking a breath, "I understand the flowers are absolutely spectacular! Certainly they won't be enjoying flowering plants at home in Newark in March! No in deedy! Hibiscus! Oh! I wonder if they'll be hibiscuses there? I absolutely *adore* hibiscus! Do you think so, Mary? Oh, I'm so pleased you are here with me! This trip just wouldn't be the same without you right here with me!"

Mary thought the poached eggs seemed to stare back up at her from their delicate, gold-rimmed bowl.

She mumbled an exhausted yet polite, "I am delighted to be here with you, too, Aunt Emily."

She, too, had not slept during the night, but it wasn't so much out of excitement. She just couldn't stop her mind from running on about so many things. Inwardly, she was still pondering her decision to make this extended excursion. This invitation to travel seemed to come up at such an opportune time; a perfect time to clear the air. The time away from her baby would be wretchedly difficult; however, she was confident she was well cared-for, safe, and secure. She would be fine with Mother, and she had a long history behind her of family members caring for their own loved-ones and infants.

And, she knew, too, that George would be fine, regardless of how he decided to spend his time. So she decided to dismiss any notion of wrongdoing on her part, and reprimanded herself about finding fault.

"I will be fine, too. I just *have* to be," she instructed herself. "Besides, this really is a wonderful time to travel, and to visit with Aunt Emily and other relatives along the way."

And, she admitted to herself, it *will* be wonderful to see Fred again. Yes, an excellent opportunity, and she intended to make the most of it.

Mary suspected that growing up as part of the Dennison family afforded her many such privileges that she would have never known had she and her mother stayed in New Orleans. Aunt Emily and Uncle Isaiah had always been so very generous, and neither she nor her mother ever wanted for anything. She pondered just how Uncle Isaiah's keen mind for business matters, his integrity, fine standing in the community, unfailing benevolence and charity, and, notwithstanding fear of God Almighty, had doubtlessly influenced her in countless ways. It was Uncle Isaiah, primarily, who instilled in her, as with his own three boys, a sense of intensity for all that life offered. She seldom sensed that same passion in others of like circumstances, though, and rarely had she found a confidant that encouraged her train of thought, or her zeal for adventure, for that matter.

The exception to that, of course, was Fred. He seemed to understand her unlike anyone else. He understood her needs and desires. Certainly, Mr. Smythe did not appear to be capable of that.

Although Mary was greatly perplexed by the circumstances she and her husband found themselves in, her thoughts reflected back to what her own dear mother must have endured. She could not even begin to comprehend how horrible it would be to suddenly find oneself a widow.

It was Sunday afternoon, November 23, 1858 when Mary's father succumbed to pneumonia. Then, before the next Sunday would dawn, her beautiful sister, Julia, was called to her eternal home as well. Only 28 months old, she, too, fell under the weight of the same symptoms of pneumonia, just as her father had merely days earlier.

This wasn't even the first loss her mother had suffered, Mary recalled. Her parents lost their only son, Raymond, a year and a half prior. So, there was Mary's weak and distraught mother, alone in New Orleans, a widow at 30, and a tiny newborn to care for. Mary, herself, was only 9 weeks old when her father and sister died. Oh! How incomprehensible that time and those circumstances must have been!

Mary could feel her heart tighten in her chest as her thoughts turned to her own husband and child.

The train's shrill whistle blared as they rocked slowly into Allegheny Station. The harsh noise seemed to echo Mary's feelings. As the B&O came to an abrupt halt, she stared out the window, not really focusing on the passengers boarding from the platform below. Tears again stung her eyes as she winced to think of the losses her mother had endured.

"What on earth am I doing?" thought Mary. "What if something horrible happens to either of them while I am away? How would I possibly manage? How would I bear it, if something were to happen to George?" Mary struggled with her thoughts.

Somehow, the idea of having left voluntarily seemed much easier to handle than the thought of having someone taken from you without volition. Why does one seem so much more justifiable, when the end result of either situation is that you are separated from one another?

"Oh! George!" Mary's heart cried.

"Mother! What had Mother done?" Mary searched for answers.

"Certainly my constitution is every bit as strong as Mother's; even stronger! Mother thought things through for herself, apparently, and managed under even more difficult circumstances. She managed very well, in fact." Mary concluded, "And so will I, regardless of the outcome of my differences with Mr. Smythe."

She thought once more of George and the baby, and then of home. Newark, that is.

"How odd." Mary mused to herself. "I'm a married woman living in Maryland and I still think of Newark as home."

Home. Aunt Emily. Uncle Isaiah. The boys. Family. Surely, if she ever needed anything, she would find it at home.

Her extended family would always see that she was well cared for and greatly loved. They would support her, regardless of what path she took or her lot in life.

"Especially Fred, he'll always see to it that I...."

The train bolted forward, startling Mary from her thoughts. Once again, they were heading west to see new things only recently appropriate for refined eastern ladies to explore, and to visit with friends and family.

And so it was. She simply had to put all this foolishness out of her mind. No matter what, she could not return home now. Aunt Emily was so excited, and Mary wouldn't be the one to cut her trip short. Aunt Emily would be so disappointed, and, if for no other reason than her sense of obligation for all she had done for her, Mary knew she must continue on her way now, for the duration of the trip.

"So be it!" Mary thought resolutely. "Why, it is 1891 after all! A woman of means is entitled to afford herself the very best that can be had, all within reason and propriety, of course. And that's precisely what I'm doing; nothing more. Why, it could even be considered my *duty* to my daughter to be as well versed in things of the world as I can be! Certainly Fredericka will even *benefit* from spending this time with her Grandmother now...and from all my experiences later. It's not as though I'm doing anything *wrong;* quite the contrary. We will all benefit from this little adventure. Aunt Emily, Ma, Fredericka...perhaps even George will develop a slightly more appreciative posture by the time I return!"

And so Mary developed her justification for leaving her husband to fend for himself and for sending her toddler to Grandmother.

"Aunt Emily is exactly right! I *must* make it a point to write to George daily—or nearly every day, as my activities and schedules permit—to tell him of all the wonderful things that we are seeing and doing!" Mary determined. "Why, once Fred joins us in Hays, Aunt Emily and I will have even more opportunities to see the sites and the countryside, and there will be so much to write to him about! I must remember to tell George to keep my letters. They will constitute an excellent travel journal and documentary that I can share with Fredericka when she's older! I'll have so much to tell her about!"

As the two well-dressed women made their way back to their private car, Mary realized that she had no idea what she'd just eaten for breakfast, or what conversation she and Aunt Emily had engaged in. Hopefully, if it were anything important, Aunt Emily would remind her later, and Mary was confident that she would.

Chapter 3

Letter One

Chicago, Ill.
March 3rd, 1891

My dear Husband,

    While waiting for our train to Rock Island, will write although Aunt Emily has already sent you a card from here. Still our time at Rock Island is so short I do not feel I ought to spend it in writing. Neither do I want to commence my first letter with yesterday's trouble, which is like a horrid nightmare. It is enough to say that we got along without attracting much attention, although I imagined every one that even glanced at me knew it all.
He[1] bid us good night then had 2 cents left. Don't know what he did with his $5 for Aunt Emily paid for dinner. All meals $1
    Well, the Limited[2] is complete in every way. Bath tub, electric lights that can be put in each section so one can read, a type-writer (which Julia had someone use for her to write to Edith[3]) & c & c. We passed through Johnstown[4] after dark. I would like to have seen it. In the paper you gave us, I see that at Yuma, Arizona they have had a fearful flood. We would have to pass through there should we visit Major Gordon[5] or Tucson. Aunt Emily seems to think she would like to visit the Fort, but I fear it would be rather too much of a trip for only one place in view. Will see what Fred says.
    I went out and took about an hour's walk and saw a little of the city,

29

although you know I have been here several times. I saw some very pretty rings in one of the large jewelry stores—quite reasonable—so thought to get it at once while I had the money. That is what Natalie[6] told me to bring her, but they hadn't any large enough in the reasonable line. However, I will buy one sometime. I got you a little article, which I think you will like. I would like to pick up some little thing in each place we stop.

Sorry to use pencil but Aunt Emily's ink is too pale. Will send this to office and then you might keep them all together if convenient.[7]

We arrived on time in a fine snow. Every baby I see makes me think of my darling.

I see they collect at 12.20 so will close with love also to James.

Your devoted wife,
M

Chapter 4

Mary was honestly relieved when, shortly after their noon meal, Aunt Emily decided to retire for an early nap. So far, the day's conversation had been as uninteresting as the endless Midwestern prairie. Usually she enjoyed their conversations, but today they seemed so shallow and worthless. Nothing they talked of held Mary's interest and her mind wandered, as it had been given to do here of late.

Much of Tuesday and Wednesday were a blur to Mary. The two-day excursion from Washington to Chicago, then Chicago to Rock Island was more exhausting than she had anticipated. Added to that were all the preparations for extended travel, and, she rather imagined, the emotional upheaval of the past several months contributed to the fatigue she was feeling. By the time the ladies reached the home of the Lyton cousins, Mary was very poor company at best.

It was wonderful to see Mark and Hannah again, and Mary was thankful for the opportunity to speak with Mark privately. She had not expected that she would divulge so much of her present situation at home, but she found it was surprisingly easy to talk with Cousin Mark. Her elder cousin by nine years, Mary always felt close to Mark even though distance prevented them from seeing each other very often. Her mother always saw to it that she knew her cousins, regardless of how far away they lived or how seldom they were able to see each other. Family had always been so important to her mother, and, although Mary got awfully tired of hearing about all of it as a child, she now better understood and appreciated the family ties.

Mary's mother, Sophia, was the seventh of the eight children, seven of whom survived to adulthood. It was Mark' parents, Margaret and

Lucas, who first cared for Mary and her mother after her father's death. As the oldest sister, Aunt Margaret assumed the initial responsibility of aiding the grieving young widow and baby. Sophia told the story many times over of the joy of seeing the entire family waiting there on the dock in Cincinnati to meet her and the baby. The trip up the River from New Orleans had been long and bitterly cold, and the widow and infant spent the remainder of the winter in Cincinnati. When spring broke, Sophia took tiny Mary to Newark where they would make their permanent home with another of Sophia's sisters and her family, Emily and her husband Isaiah. Mary was nurtured in the love of her extended family and grew up in their home beside her cousins. She enjoyed a lavish and pampered childhood and spent all of her days there prior to her marriage to George Smythe.

Mary pondered how her life would have been different had they stayed in Cincinnati rather than going east to Newark. Mark would be more like a brother, she thought, but cousin he is, and it was very good to talk with him.

"He's close enough to care about my future, but distant enough to have an objective point of view." Or so Mary thought.

Aunt Emily opted not to take a sleigh ride through the countryside, but rather to stay in and visit with Hannah. That provided a perfect opportunity for Mark and Mary to talk. He was certainly surprised that George and Mary were at an impasse, but instructed her in no uncertain terms to remain true to her vows, and to the family's strong values and integrity. He made it all sound so very clear and simple: Enjoy the time away, and then return to George with a fresh perspective and renewed devotion. Be the wife that George needed her to be. Temper her will in favor of his. Do not even entertain thoughts that would be divisive. Set a good example for Fredericka and raise her to be a kind, loving woman, who will, in turn, be devoted to her husband.

And that was that. Just as Aunt Emily had, Mark too reminded Mary of George's love for her.

"Odd," she puzzled, "how that seems so obvious to everyone but me."

Chapter 5

Letter Two

St. Joseph, Missouri
March 6th 1891

Have written, dearest, nearly every day for Aunt Emily says postals are better than nothing. Have not heard from you yet; it is now Friday and it seems long since Monday, but I hope to hear when we reach Kansas City tomorrow evening. We leave here tomorrow 2:25 P.M., so there is a chance of hearing from you here.

Well, we had a grand visit with Cousin Mark. He and Hannah each expressed a desire to have you visit them. Mark met us with his carriage; a very nice low one that Aunt Emily could get into easily. He has a fine pair of horses. They also keep a cow. Their home is beautiful; a large stone house right on the river bank. Hannah has it arranged quite artistically. They keep two servants, besides the man. We reached there after eight. The boys were all up to see us, and Hannah had a nice warm tea awaiting us. The children are so nice. Mark Jr. is in the High School; he takes great interest in birds, and their Harvey's mind turns to butterflies. Their collections are quite interesting and William is very happy with his stamps. The three boys have very nice books for them. By the way, when you have any stamps you don't need, enclose one or a few as I have been using Aunt Emily's.

While on Rock Island, we had a sleigh-ride. Went to see the changes. Mark took me through the shops; I kept wishing for you, my darling, for I knew you would have enjoyed it and would have understood better than I did. We left there 11:30 p.m. Mar. 4th. Took the sleeper direct here. Took a carriage right here. They all are lovely. Mr. & Mrs. Forge are about seventy. There is one daughter home; she teaches. Then, two married daughters came home to be here while we were here and the other married one lived near where we all go tonight to tea. You would be just delighted with them all! The two girls who are home on a visit have each a child with them. One is 20 months old and acts just like my darling Fredericka has for the last 2 weeks. Wants the Mama.

Have had a letter from home and they seem to think it might have been wise had we coaxed JBR[8] back to New York. We are anxious to learn what has been done in the case.

We are to stop with Mrs. Dr. Hart's sister[9] in Kansas City, but I expect to see Kate R.[10]

Write to Denver. No, I fear I would not get it. We will spend Sunday a week in Sacramento and will inquire at general delivery there.

Love to James and, more than love to you my dearest George.

Your devoted wife

What is Miss Lizzie R's cousins' name in Pasadena? Never mind; I find I have it.

Chapter 6

Letter Three

2821 E 6ᵗʰ St.
Kansas City, MO
Sunday afternoon, March 8ᵗʰ, 1891

Well, darling, so far on our trip in safety. We left St. Joe at 2:30 p.m. yesterday; reached here at 6:00 p.m. in a snowstorm.

This is a beautiful house, but, as they keep but one servant, it isn't kept up to quite the point you would consider was right. Mrs. Gill is, as you know, Mrs. Hart's sister. Kentucky women, and they, I imagine, don't pretend to be model housekeepers. However, she is as nice as can be and I feel so at home; a much more desirable thing than fearing to move a thing as one feels in some homes. We have her daughter's room, Mrs. Beecher, who is away. You know, Mr. and Mrs. Beecher visited Aunt Emily this fall with a 15 months baby girl, who they lost one week after returning west. A large picture of the little thing stands in one corner; her little shoes and toys are also around. I should think it would only make them feel worse. None of them can mention the little creature without crying. They think our baby beautiful.

This morning I went to church with Mr. & Mrs. Gill. They attend the Presbyterian Church. I enjoyed their pastor Dr. Neal very much. After dinner (which was a splendid one!) Kate R.[11] called and has just gone. She is as sad as ever and the brother-in-law I half thought might be interested in her is to be married again next fall, so, you see, I imagined wrong, but I didn't even hint at such a thing. It would have been much out of place seeing how sad she was. She told me she was in a store and has charge of some department. I didn't quite catch it and didn't like to ask. She wanted to be remembered to you. She told Mrs. Gill her visit with us was such a bright spot. She is in deep mourning.

We did enjoy our St. Joe visit so much! Mr. Forge's daughters are all lovely. The home of Hannah Shireman where we took tea on Friday, as I wrote you, is very nice and I liked her husband so much. She is a good housekeeper, as I imagine the other girls are.

A Mr. Wolcott came to Kansas City on our train and helped us also in changing our tickets & c. He is engaged to a Miss Olivia Barne; a cousin of the Forge girls. They showed us the house where Jesse James was captured, and, as we went through Parkville, Missouri, Mr. Wolcott pointed out Park College.

I suppose you hear more than we do about Joshua[12] so won't repeat.

How I would love to see you this afternoon. I wonder how my other darling (baby) is. Is Natalie home yet? How have you and James gotten along?

Maybe you had best ask Ma if Fredericka needs anything. I know how to manage with what I had, but some were old.

Will not mail this till morning. Mr. Gill is a lawyer and Mr. Beecher is connected with the smelting works. Send next to San Francisco General Delivery. Thanks for list.

Chapter 7

Monday, March 9

What a spectacularly glorious morning! Mary closed her eyes and smiled as she sat up in bed and plumped the many billowy pillows around her petite frame. The bright morning sun shown in through the oversized windows, casting delicate lacey-curtain shadows on the opposite wall. She pulled the pink silk duvet close up under her chin and snuggled deep down under.

"This is going to be such a wonderful day!" she smiled as she thought to herself. "Oh! I'm so thankful for a peaceful night's rest, finally! It seems so long since I've slept well and awoke feeling refreshed and ready for the day!"

Mary must have nodded off, as she was startled by the slight little knock on the bedroom door. Permission given, Mrs. Gill entered.

"Good morning, dear! Did you sleep well?" Without waiting a reply, she continued. I'm so sorry to disturb you, but you have mail. It appears to be a letter from George, and I knew you'd want it delivered without delay. Take your time in coming downstairs, dear. Your breakfast will be served whenever you are ready."

With that, her hostess handed Mary the letter and tiptoed out the door.

The "clack" of the closing door latch echoed through the enormous room.

Mary stared at the envelope: a letter from George. She recalled that it was only a week ago today that they parted company in Washington. That seems so long ago now, so many miles, so many tears…They were both so very angry…Mary wasn't even sure he'd write at all, and was pleasantly surprised.

She tore open the seal, and scanned quickly for word of the baby…

"…all was well at home…James is there with him…and so is Natalie…he is fine…."

Here! Here's word! He "…put Mother and Fredericka on the train to return to Newark on Tuesday morning without incident."

Mary scoured that part again for details. She reread that part. He "…put Mother and Fredericka on the train to Newark Tuesday morning without incident."

That means Mother only stayed one night after I left, before returning home to New Jersey, Mary realized. She continued on, "…without incident." What in blazes name does that mean? Things must have been tense otherwise Mother would have stayed on longer in Hyattsville. She so much loved to show off Fredericka to her Maryland and Washington friends!

Fredericka.

Tears welled up in Mary's eyes at the thought of her baby girl. Her precious baby girl.

Mary let her hand and the letter drop limp to the billowy comforter below, and she just sobbed.

"It's going to be so hard to be away from her" she struggled. "If I were not convinced that this time away were so important, why, I could almost think I were doing the wrong thing."

"I certainly can't dwell on that," she reprimanded herself, picked up the letter, and read on.

"George's work at the post office keeps him busy, and he says he thinks of me daily as he takes the train into town from Hyattsville."

"That's romantic." She snarled to herself. "I wonder if he thinks of me otherwise or just as he travels with a multitude of strangers?"

He says he "…misses me and for me to enjoy my travels". "With love to Aunt Emily", he closes the letter, with the words, "Yours always, George".

Well, at least he wrote, Mary settled. She hadn't been at all sure he would. There is certainly no reason for him *not* to write. After all, I am his *wife*.

With that, she rolled out of bed and prepared for her day ahead.

It was only as she faced her extensive wardrobe that she began to admit to herself just how anxious she was about being reunited with Fred tonight. Although the two cousins had written, they had seen each other infrequently since January 27, 1887. That was the day Mary became Mrs. George M. Smythe.

It was a small, elegant ceremony in Aunt Emily and Uncle Isaiah's home where Mary Stevenson and George Smythe took their wedding vows. Mary held her breath throughout the entire ceremony in anticipation of Fred's (or someone else's) expressed objection. However, objections having not come, their vows were completed, obligations defined, commitments begun. Despite his horror at the thought of Mary's marriage to George, Fred stood silently and dutifully as an official witness to their nuptials.

From the moment Mary first told Fred of their meeting, he objected to her relationship with George. As their affection grew for one another, so did Fred's disapproval and disdain. At times, his emotion even bordered on rage. He was adamant that Mary was simply enamored with the rather fine figure Mr. Smythe presented in his Signal Corps uniform. Or, that her romantic heart was flattered by George's smooth words (although Fred never knew the half of it!). Or, infuriatingly enough, he even dared imply that perhaps Mary was feeling a tad desperate, given her age.

"How dare Fred make such implications," she thought. "No, I truly love George," she argued.

With each heated discussion Fred and Mary engaged in, she became more determined to go her own way, to marry George Smythe, if, for no other reason, than to prove Fred wrong.

The five huge steamer trunks held a multitude of ensemble possibilities, but nothing seemed right for this special occasion. Mary quickly ruled out the yellow brocade. "Fred always said yellow made me look 'sallow,'" Mary mumbled to herself.

The mint green taffeta was entirely too spring-like for a snowy March night. The Champaign-colored brocade with the hand-embroidered tapestry sash just wouldn't do either. She considered the powder blue French silk with the billowing ecru lace but decided to save that for a special evening later on. The navy skirt and white blouse made her look like a schoolmarm. The burgundy and sage floral was so utilitarian. She rooted through and tossed other possibilities aside in frustration.

"Why on earth is this so important?" Mary blurted out loud to no one other than herself.

Mary plopped down hard on the moss green velvet sofa. She ran her fingers through the button-tufted folds on the circular center back section. The hand-carved mahogany frame made this a lovely piece, but the intricacies of the wood held dust.

Mary blinked hard in an effort to hold back the tears. It did not help.

These tears were not over missing the baby or even anger at George. These were Fred's tears. They certainly aren't the first, nor did she suspect the last.

"It has been so very long since Fred and I have been together, and tonight I'll see him again." The thought made her tremble to her very core. Mary's thoughts completely overwhelmed her.

"What do I do with this multitude of feelings, now that we are merely hours away from being in each other's presence? A genuine excitement grips my very being that I, somehow, have been able to suppress until this very moment," she realized.

"Now the time is approaching, and I must try to face the reality that I am truly thrilled about seeing him; about being near him; the possibility of even the slightest glancing touch...."

Her thoughts wandered to allow her to think the unimaginable.

"Would time and distance erase—or only serve to magnify—what we once felt for each other?"

Mary's mind was an uncontrollable jumble.

"I can only wonder what he's thinking right now. Does he long to see me? Has he even thought of me with any frequency? Does he want to be with me? Does he want to hold me, as he once wanted so desperately? On the other hand, will he regard me as his 'married cousin, Mrs. Smythe' and not even afford me the courtesy of a family embrace or kiss on the cheek? What would I then do?"

With that thought in mind, Mary's choice was suddenly crystal clear.

"It will be the rose pink silk with the bodice of ivory Belgian lace! Fred always loved to see me in shades of rose and pink…makes me have a 'natural healthy and rosy glow', he always said. And I know this gown *does* make my waist look tiny and my eyes a richer brown. I know I look good in this gown, so this it shall be!"

Mary was thrilled with her choice, and, with that decision made, she jumped up off the davenport and rooted for her very loveliest foundations.

"This reunion will be *wonderful*!" Mary delighted. "I just know it will be!"

Chapter 8

Letter Four

Monday A M

Dearest,

    Yours of Thursday just received. Also letters from home and one from Lydia[13] giving full acct. Will send it to you in my next. Poor girl. She appreciates so much what you and the others have done for her.
    It is about time for the carriage to move us to our train. We meet Fred at 7:30 p.m.

Ever Yours
M

Chapter 9

It was a bitterly cold and blustery day in January when Mary received the letter from Aunt Emily. She had written to invite Mary to be her guest on a three or four month travel excursion to California. The plan was to meet in Washington, DC, and, from there, to travel throughout the country, visiting relatives and old family friends along the way. The day her letter arrived, an intense northeast storm gripped much of the mid-Atlantic seaboard. It was fearfully cold and the area was having snow for the third day in a row.

Mary felt as though only her marriage to George Smythe was colder than the wind that howled outside. Winter had set in, and all looked very bleak.

With the arrival of Aunt Emily's invitation came hope, and an excellent excuse to leave the difficulties at home. Although Mary pondered the exciting idea, no lady of proper upbringing would even entertain the thought of leaving her husband, even on a temporary arrangement. With Aunt Emily's timely invitation, however, Mary could travel as her companion, and that would at least do something to reduce the scorn and ridicule she was certain to encounter. It was a near-perfect plan, and California sounded *so* inviting!

Mary made her decision and informed her husband.

He was livid.

"You are my *wife* and your place is here with me!" he shouted, "and with your daughter. Not on some train traipsing all over the country!"

"Why, George Smythe! It almost seems as though you actually care about what I do."

"Mary!" he snapped. Then, in a more controlled tone, "Mary," he said softly as he moved in her direction. "Mary, I *do* care. I love you…more than I can tell you. I admit I don't always show it, but I do love you, and I do care about you."

"My mind's made up, George" she said bluntly, as she turned her back to him. "I'm going away with Aunt Emily for a little respite. Mother will keep the baby."

"You won't, Mary! This is nonsense! Completely out of the question. The idea is absurd!" he bellowed. "Besides, I'd be frantic thinking of the two of you women alone. How can you think of it?"

"Only as far as Hays, George." Mary responded in a very curt tone. "Fred will join us there. He's speculating on an orange grove in California and wants to see it for himself," Mary stated as matter-of-factly as she could.

"I see," said George. He was immediately disheartened. "How very convenient."

"George!" Mary snapped back, and then caught herself.

It was best left alone and unspoken, for George knew very well all the feelings that were involved. He knew just how much Fred disapproved of him and of their marriage. He was also keenly aware of the degree to which Fred was devoted to Mary.

And, Mary knew, he suspected at least, that but for the fact that Mary and Fred were cousins it was probable they would have entertained the idea of marriage.

Mary was momentarily stung by how painful and difficult this announcement must be for George. Granted, their marriage had grown cold and lifeless, but Mary was sure he wasn't expecting anything like this. George always felt Fred was an obstacle to overcome and he had battled that unseen wall for more than four years now. Sometimes those battles were victorious; sometimes not so much so.

Such was the case when Mary insisted that the happy couple name their first-born child 'Fredericka Dennison Smythe,' very pointedly to honor Cousin Frederick Dennison. George complied. Why, he was so thrilled with his new baby girl, that Mary could have called her just about anything as far as he was concerned. Nevertheless, it was George who bore the brunt of it when more than one proper Victorian eyebrow was raised in disgust. Mary was equally sure that this trip of hers would elicit the same such responses.

"Never mind that; he'll just have to handle it. His shoulders are broad." Mary reasoned. "This is my life, and I shall do precisely as I wish, not as society dictates."

"George" Mary said softly. "You know I love you. I have since the day I met you. I just feel so overwhelmed with responsibilities…and so alone so much of the time. I just need some time away…time to think."

"What's there to think about, Mary? You are my wife, and Fredericka's mother. Your place is here with us."

"I know, I know, George. I'm not sure I can explain it to you."

With that, he looked down and slowly walked out of the room. He knew her mind was made up and there was no further use to discuss the matter.

Chapter 10

"I have only fooled myself if I thought my motives in traveling were to unselfishly escort Aunt Emily on her trip," Mary finally admitted to herself, "or even to give George and me time to sort out our differences."

Last night was certainly proof of that. Mary's yearning just to see Fred once again was finally fulfilled, and she was not disappointed.

As the train rocked and screeched to a stop in Hays, the gas lamps mixed with the late evening moonlight to illuminate Fred's silhouette standing on the platform. Aunt Emily and Mary gathered their immediate belongings, and the porter assisted them in alighting from the train.

Mary stood aside and slightly behind Aunt Emily as Fred greeted his mother and hugged her warmly. Mary watched as he softly kissed her cheek, hugged her again, then, holding her gently by the shoulders looked carefully into her face.

"You look *wonderful*, Mother," he said, and hugged her again. Over her shoulder, Fred's eyes met Mary's.

Mary's anxious heart thundered as she waited to see what reception she would receive. Tears welled in her eyes in anticipation and anxiety. She thought her chest would burst within her.

Gently backing away from his mother's embrace, Fred turned to Mary.

He stood silently for an endless instant, then, slowly and deliberately, he moved toward her.

Mary smiled faintly and extended both hands out to him in front of her tiny waist.

With a great sigh, Fred gathered her gloved hands up in his own and drew them to his lips. Pressing his lips upon the back of her hands, he kissed them over and over as he fixed his gaze on his dear Mary.

His piercing brown eyes immediately and completely enthralled her. He looked at Mary as if she were the only person in the world, and Mary's heart melted. Her heart was enraptured.

"Mary! My precious, precious Mary!" he spoke ever so softly as he wrapped her in his arms. He gently kissed her ear as he whispered with a deep sigh, "I've missed you so desperately...."

In those first few seconds, all the time that had passed vanished in an instant.

Mary knew right then, that, although everything was different, nothing at all had changed.

Cousin Frederick Dennison
c. 1891

Pullman Dining Car Service.

SUPPER.

Oatmeal with Cream

Raw Oysters   Stewed Oysters

Broiled White Fish

Broiled Ham   Boneless Bacon

Tenderloin Steak, Plain, with Mushrooms or Tomato Sauce

Mutton Chops, Plain, or with Tomato Sauce

EGGS: Boiled,   Fried,   Shirred,   Scrambled

Omelette, Plain, with Ham, Parsley, Jelly or Rum

Baked Potatoes   German Fried   Stewed

Cold Roast Beef   Beef Tongue

Sardines   Pickled Lambs Tongue   Cold Ham

Boston Baked Beans   Baked Sweet Potatoes

Cold Slaw

Vienna Bread   Graham Bread   Tea Biscuit

Dry Toast   Buttered Toast   Dipped Toast

Graham, and Oatmeal Wafers

California Table Fruit

Coffee   Chocolate   Mixed Tea   Milk

Waffles with Maple Syrup

MEALS, SEVENTY-FIVE CENTS.

TABLE WATER FROM THE ELLIS SPRINGS, KANSAS.

My dear Geo

Mailed you a letter yesterday from
U.C. our journey to Hays was pleasant. had
agreeable people on board enjoyed a splendid
dinner & tea in the dining car the Superintendent
of which gave me the full set of bills of
fare guess I'd better not send them to you for
fear they might not compare well with yours
but will save all such things to show you.
Fred & May boarded the car at 8.30 & looks
well. We reached here at 7.30 this a.m.
Have had a good breakfast & now while
Aunt M is taking a nap & Fred has gone out
to see about the sections for tomorrow
night & the P.O. where we may have
letters I will write as he said he would
take me out when he returned. The first
thing I saw this morn was Pikes Peak covered
with snow it was 100 & some miles off. looked
like a big cloud in the blue sky. it is quite

Chapter 11

Letter Five

The Albany Hotel[14]
Denver, CO
Tuesday, March 10, 1891

My Dear George,

Mailed you a letter yesterday from Kansas City. Our journey to Hays was pleasant. Had agreeable people on board. Enjoyed a splendid dinner and tea in the dining car, the superintendent of which gave me the full set of bills of fare. Guess I'd better not send them to you for fear they might not compare well with yours, but will save all such things to show you. Fred & Max[15] boarded the car at 8:30. Fred looks well. We reached here at 7:30 this A.M. Have had a good breakfast, and now, while Aunt Emily is taking a nap and Fred has gone out to see about the sections for tomorrow night and to the P.O. where we may have letters, I will write, as he said he would take me out when he returned.

The first thing I saw this morn was Pikes Peak covered with snow. It was 100 and some miles off. Looked like a big cloud in the blue sky. It is quite warm here as I look out our window (see marked)[16]. I notice many gentlemen without overcoats.

Tell Mrs. Ungerford[17] I thought of her when going through Ellsworth and that all the places seem to have grown. Give her love *also to Mrs. Anderson*[18]. *I will write to her soon. What did she say about the cage, and what did Mr. Dunnton*[19] *say about the paper?*

Ask Natalie to please take off the cover to your card table. So much light will fade it. Also, please get her to put the camphor in my box of furs which is under the silver case. Don't forget to put some in washstand closet and in your full-dress suit. Want to write Miss Lizzie R. and others this A.M., so will stop on this for awhile. I want to write Natalie. Where shall I direct?

This is a live city!

The boy has just handed in an invitation to each of us to attend an opening. Received a letter from Mrs. Patterson here. Direct next to Palace Hotel, San Francisco. Will send for Sacramento mail to be forwarded.

Lovingly,
M

Chapter 12

"Why, Frederick! If they think so highly of us as to extend an invitation to us, then we simply *must* attend!" Aunt Emily declared in an almost-raised voice. "We absolutely *must* attend!"

"Mother, they can't '...think so highly of us'! They don't even know us. It was merely an invitation of courtesy. What they *do* know is that we are staying in the finest suites and will, hopefully, travel this way again. At the very least, they want us to tell our friends of their fine, new hotel. I'm quite certain it has nothing to do with 'us' personally, I assure you," Fred stated very matter-of-factly as he poured himself another cup of coffee.

"Well, no matter. We've only just arrived in Denver, Frederick. What on earth could possibly be more important than a gala at a fine new establishment? Why, it will be great fun! And *dinner!* Can you imagine, Frederick? The very finest of *everything*, I'm sure! Oh! It will be just lovely! Yes, we'll all go! What shall I wear? Oh, never mind that, now. I'm sure I will find something. Or *shopping!* Perhaps Mary and I shall slip out after lunch. Better yet, we'll call for a carriage, *dine out*, then *shop! Oh, yes!* I wonder if they'll be a sampling of all of that wild game we hear so much about...."

"Mother!" Fred interrupted the monologue that he knew could run on for some time. "I have other plans."

"*Other plans!* "Why, what 'other plans', for heavens sake?" Aunt Emily almost demanded an answer of her son.

"I've arranged a private dinner for Mary and me here at the Albany. I've gone to great lengths, and won't change a thing for some unexpected hotel event."

"I see." His disheartened mother replied in a tone that he recognized.

"Oh, Mother. I'll work *something* out. I'll see to it that you attend the dinner." Fred said with a deep sigh. He was slightly exasperated with this unanticipated need to adjust plans. "Just let me think on it a while" he said.

"Oh, I know you will, dear! You always do work things out! Just let me know what time I need to be ready, and I shall be. I promise not to keep you waiting, dear."

With that assurance, Aunt Emily bustled briskly to her suite to prepare for her day out in Denver.

Fred cared little whether it was a brilliant idea on his part or if it was Divine intervention, but his solution to the dilemma was nearly perfect.

On the train from Kansas City to Denver, Aunt Emily made the acquaintance of a lovely woman, a Mrs. Amanda Williams. Even though she was from somewhere on the prairie, she was traveling first class, and appeared to be of the finest caliber. The two women seemed to chat comfortably right from the start. Upon finding that Mrs. Williams was staying in the hotel suite adjacent to his mother's, and considering that the she was traveling unescorted (except for her maid, of course), it seemed only proper to invite her to dine with his mother in his stead. He would arrange a carriage to pick up the ladies at the Albany for the short trip to the lavish new hotel. He would send Max along, who would wait with the other valets and call a carriage when the ladies were ready to return.

Mrs. Williams thought it only too kind of Frederick to forego his own invitation in order to provide his mother with the companionship of a new-found friend.

She nearly jumped with excitement as she said, "Oh! You are *such* a thoughtful young man, Frederick! No wonder your Mother is so proud of you! Indeed, she raised you so well! I kindly accept your invitation, and shall gladly accompany your mother to dinner this evening" Mrs. Williams replied in a soft, sweet voice. "I shall await your driver at six. Meanwhile, do you suppose your Mother would care to shop this afternoon? I hear Denver has *fine* millenaries! Oh! Of course you wouldn't know! Either, that is…about whether your mother would like to shop *or* about Denver's fine millenaries! How silly of me! I'll just tap on the door to her suite and ask her myself! Perhaps we could take our noon meal out as well!"

With that dialog, Mrs. Williams scurried off, leaving Fred all the more confidant that he had created a perfect match.

And he was free to spend the evening alone with Mary.

Chapter 13

After an anxious day, Mary met Fred downstairs in the grand foyer of the Albany Hotel just a few minutes before seven. He had arranged for a private dining room where the two cousins would enjoy a fine, leisurely dinner and pleasant conversation.

The Albany was most accommodating, and the meal superb. From the finest of Champaign to one of her favorite desserts, everything was perfect. Fresh seafood had surely presented a logistical challenge for the Albany, but Fred saw to it that the evening included all of Mary's favorite delicacies. Even the fresh flowers that filled the intimate room contained prized deep blue Delphinium and Baby's Breath; not an easy task in Denver in March. Mary knew this evening cost Fred an untold fortune, as he had spared no detail.

It was early in the evening, over the tomato-basil bisque, that Fred redirected their conversation abruptly from casual reminiscing to his intended purpose. Although he chose his words carefully, he was clear. He expressed how devastated he had been when Mary chose to marry George, and how distraught he had been these last four long years. He had attempted to court other ladies but quickly broke off each relationship. He said he had never loved anyone else, and never would.

Mary sat silently, although she was certain the pounding of her heart could be seen as well as heard. She sipped from the silver soupspoon a tiny bit at a time, and slowly picked through her salad, nudging the thinly sliced onions and cucumbers off to the side of her salad plate.

Fred began by reminding Mary of the many times, prior to her engagement to George, when he had escorted her to social functions, and the great fun that they always enjoyed. He talked about how the two of them, even as children, always seemed to think similar thoughts and understood each other's deepest feelings. He reminded her of how they both cherished their family and of the loved-ones they both cared so deeply for. Then he assured Mary of his great love and unrelenting devotion for her and her alone.

"Fred! Stop! Please! George is my *husband!*" Mary dropped her salad fork with somewhat of a clatter. She could take it no more.

"You know you are not happy with that man, Mary. You never will be. He's a cad. You deserve better, and I can give you anything your heart desires."

Fred's words almost seemed rehearsed.

"Fred," Mary began slowly and deliberately. "George is a good man; really he is. I've just been frustrated, recently, that's all. George has never laid a hand on me in anger. You know I've always wished he imbibed less, but I knew that was a concern when I agreed to become his wife."

"It has sounded to me, in all your letters, that you have been more than a little 'frustrated', and that it hasn't just been recently," Fred retorted.

"Well," she began very carefully, "he has, perhaps, on occasion forgotten his responsibilities as a husband and father, and has not always come home directly from work. Sometimes it has been well into the early hours of the morning when he returns home. That always worries me so." Mary paused for a sip of tea. "And, certainly, there is no discussion or explanation of those times, and that just infuriates me further," she said flatly.

Of course, none of this was news to Fred. Mary's life-long confidant, she'd written him at least weekly since leaving home. Unbeknownst to her, though, her detailed correspondences were merely serving to convince Fred all the more that her rightful place was with him, and not with George Smythe.

And, for the next ten weeks, she would be.

After a truly fine dinner, Fred called for a carriage. He wouldn't tell Mary what he had in mind, out of fear that she would protest. He knew her well enough though to know that she was always up for an adventure and that with just a little persuasion he would have her out the door.

The opulent new Majestic Hotel was all it was billed to be and the Grand Ballroom glistened with fresh gold gilt. The expansive new marble floor was polished to such a high luster as to cause some couple's footing to be unsure. Fred and Mary, however, confidently sailed gracefully and elegantly around the cavernous room, dancing late into the night.

The diminutive Mary was stunningly beautiful in her powder blue gown. Its yards of fine French silk engulfed her tiny figure but did not overpower her. The slightest movement of her agile frame sent the silk in a single, fluid motion, perfectly timed to the orchestra's music. She was glad she had chosen this night to wear her special gown.

"Such a lovely couple." was heard murmured by more than one spectator, and, indeed, they were. Other couples stepped aside while all focused their attention on Mary and Fred.

For a fleeting moment, Mary wondered if anyone knew that they were not husband and wife. She knew her ample diamond rings glistened for all to see that she was a married woman.

Mary quickly dismissed the thought, for it did not matter. At this moment, nothing mattered. She was in another world—in Fred's arms—dancing away the night.

His strong, broad hand on the small of her back guided her effortlessly in perfect rhythm. Hour after hour he held her close, gazing lovingly into her deep eyes. He drew her very near...so near, in fact, that she could feel his soft, warm breath on her ear...on her neck...

Little did she realize just a few hours earlier when she had written George telling him that 'an invitation had been received,' that it would prove to be such an incredibly sensual evening.

Chapter 14

"Tomato juice," he said flatly as he snapped shut his little black leather medical bag. "Tomato juice. In small sips. Slow, deep breaths of fresh air when she's up to it; otherwise, let her rest as much as she will."

The doctor's raised eyebrows and gruff manner conveyed his disapproval at being summoned with such a panic over this non life-threatening disturbance.

"*Tomato juice!*" Fred exclaimed in disbelief. It was obvious from his tone of voice that he seriously questioned the physician's prescription—and his credibility. "The dear woman is wretchedly ill, and you prescribe 'fresh air and *tomato juice*? Preposterous!" Fred raged.

"Sir, please! Mrs. Smythe has been overtaken with an ailment known as 'altitude sickness,' nothing more, nothing less. I see this quite often these days, and it is especially common in genteel women from the east. Tomato juice will help to settle her stomach. Slow, deep breathing will help her acclimate to the difference in our air here. And one more thing, sir. I would strongly suggest you temper the dancing, gaiety, and champagne."

With that word of caution and implied disapproval, the finest doctor in all of Denver—not to mention the finest money could afford—left the room and closed the door behind him.

Chapter 15

Letter Six

One of highest points of the continent
In Rocky Mts. 10 A.M. 3-12-91

Wrote a postal from Cheyenne. We have just passed a place called Sherman on Summit. There was a large pyramid built of stone with a slab and a head cut in[20]. It is to commemorate Sherman's march to sea or his other battles. Now we have reached Laramie. It seems like quite a place!

We have the drawing room, so you see how comfortable we are. A private toilet room connected with it.

It was so sad. In the next section to us last night was a gentleman with his dear little 4 month-old baby. Its Mama died on Friday, he told me. He is now in the car ahead. How I would love to take care of it. Its cry would go right to my heart and I could not keep the tears back. Some days, when I think of my precious baby, I have to fight very hard not to break down. When we are passing homes and I see the little clothes blowing on the lines, oh, how it makes me long to hold my darling to my heart. I don't let Aunt Emily or Fred know how the sight of a child goes through and through me, for they are so lovely to me and I am having the very best the land can offer. But, oh, how I wish I could divide it with you my dear, dear husband. But I must not write in this strain, for it is not giving you any pleasure, you who are so good to me. Everything is covered with a light snow and every little way there are things that look like fences called snow breaks. Sometimes there will be 4 or 5 lines set back of each other. We have been through two snow sheds

(Mary's letter ends abruptly here.)

63

Chapter 16

Late Wednesday afternoon the coachman arrived, precisely at the time Fred had prearranged, to move the unusual entourage from the Albany to the train station. A powdery, fine snow began to blanket the city and muffle the street noises of the busy downtown district. The multitude of steamer trunks, combined with the slow pace of the thoroughly green and queasy Mrs. Smythe, complicated the logistics and lengthened the estimated transport time. Mary knew Fred was impatient but was impressed that he maintained his gentlemanly composure. As soon as the travelers settled into their designated quarters, the train pulled out of the station, and it was only a few minutes behind its posted schedule.

For once Mary realized how privileged she was, and was thankful for her first-class accommodations. For a fleeting moment, she thought of how wretched it would be to be this ill and relegated to coach. With that thought quickly dismissed as "unimaginable," she poured herself another cup of tea in the plush comfort of her private drawing room.

The journey from Denver to San Francisco would take the better part of Wednesday to midday Saturday. The passage through the Rocky Mountains would be slow and snowy, and would reveal breathtakingly beautiful scenery. The majestic and awesome grandeur of the mountains would provide a spectacular backdrop for Mary to be alone with her thoughts, and the strong-willed beauty's thoughts were as unsettled as her stomach.

Her relentless altitude sickness and persistent queasiness, combined with the natural movement of the train, gave her a perfect excuse to be alone. She needed desperately to be alone, and even Aunt Emily encouraged her to do so. She gently instructed Mary to "…rest; sleep as much as you can…," but she was not sleeping and rest did not come easily. Her mind raced and it seemed she could not focus on any one thing. She was exhausted. What troubled her more than anything, though, was the realization that not only were her thoughts unsettled, but her heart was equally so.

Mary queried herself repeatedly. "What happened…what in heaven's name happened Tuesday night?"

Mary was taken aback and confused by the many emotions elicited by her evening with Fred. Although her relationship with her husband was strained to say the least, she was not prepared for the flood of feelings she was suddenly dealing with. Something like a passion, which she had not felt in months or years, was sparked when Fred held her that close. And, problematically, she very much liked what she felt.

Over and over she recalled his strong hand holding her tiny frame close as they swayed rhythmically to the grand orchestra's music. She could still feel his warm breath on her ear as he told her of his love and of his hopes for their future. At the time, she just melted more into his arms and loved every minute of it.

Now, for the first time in her pampered life, she was genuinely afraid of what she was feeling, and these feelings were as foreign and unfamiliar as the passing countryside.

A brisk rap on the parlor door startled her from her jumbled thoughts. "Mary, darling?" It was Fred's deep, confident voice. "Mary, I've come to check on you. How are you feeling, dear?"

Mary arose from the wine-colored velvet tufted sofa, wrapped herself in her silk robe, and padded to the door. She opened the door just wide enough to reveal her caller holding a silver tray with hot tea and toast.

"Fred." she began flatly, but was interrupted. She exhaled a heavy sigh as Fred began to speak.

"My dear, you're looking much better this afternoon!" Fred began, as he started past her with the tray. "I thought you would enjoy a fresh pot of tea…I'll just set it here." With that, he set the tray on the carved oval mahogany table over near the window.

"I would have called the attendant for tea." Mary was very surprised at the tone of her own voice. "You did not need to bring it yourself, Fred."

"Oh, it was no bother, and I wanted to check on you myself," he replied. He approached Mary, still standing by the doorway. "Do you feel up to visiting for a bit, dear?"

"No, Fred, I'm afraid I really don't. Please leave." Her own words startled her, and dumbfounded the young man. Neither could recall a time when they did not want to be in each other's company, so this was certainly a first.

"Mary, what's wrong, dear?" Fred inquired in a very disheartened tone of voice.

"Fred, I'm just ill, and I can't talk right now." Mary paused. "I don't know myself 'what's wrong', and I just need to be left alone. Please."

He stared at her, absolutely speechless. "Mary," he finally began, "just let me sit quietly with you. I won't press you, dear."

"No, I really need for you to leave now, Fred," and she opened the door a little wider.

"Will you join us for dinner this evening?" he inquired in an adjusted tone.

"I have no idea if I'll be up to it." Mary replied flatly, as he walked through the door.

"I see," he said. "If you don't join us for dinner, I'll have Max check on your welfare before retiring this evening." With that, Fred quietly disappeared down the Pullman's long, swaying corridor.

And, once again, Mary's emotions surfaced. It only took one glance at his deep brown eyes and a word from his sensual voice to rouse the feelings she was so desperately trying to dismiss. It was then she was struck with the realization that she would be with this man for the next ten weeks, and, regardless of what she tried to convince herself, she was desperately in love with him.

In addition, her husband was nearly 3,000 miles away.

Chapter 17

After Fred left her private room, Mary cried herself to sleep. She was in agony over the turmoil she was experiencing and hated that she could not simply assess the situation and deal with the facts as she was so accustomed to doing. This was something different, and she feared she had met her match.

She awoke just in time to decide about dinner. She simply had to pull herself together and join the others for dinner, even if she had nothing more than tea. She couldn't stay in her sleeper for the duration of the trip, nor would she miss the opportunities at hand. She again approached her multitude of apparel choices, and this time decided to go with the conservative and plain skirt and blouse...the one that made her feel like a very proper and modest schoolteacher. The choice was easier this time.

"We are so pleased you feel up to joining us!" Aunt Emily exclaimed as Mary arrived at the table slightly after the others. "Oh, you are looking so much better! Did you nap, dear? Naps do wonders! I absolutely *love* my naps! I just love to get all cozy under the duvet and snuggle deep down into billowy pillows! You know, I never understood why old people loved their naps so much, but now it seems perfectly natural! I wonder if I am officially old, now that I love my naps, too?" she quizzed. "Anyway, dear, I am so glad you are with us! Fresh-killed ruffled grouse! I hear they were shot right from the train! Have you heard that some men were hunting right from the train? Isn't this a lark! What do you feel like, dear? Does anything sound good to you?" Aunt Emily hardly took a breath.

Mary, however, took a very deep breath, and letting it out said, "Perhaps just a little broth would be fine, please."

"Oh, yes, wise choice, dear! Fred, what about you, son? What sounds good to you this evening? You can have *anything* your heart desires!"

His dark eyes shot across the table to meet Mary's, and he didn't hear another word his mother said the entire evening.

Fred, too, knew he was just as in love with Mary as he had ever been. He could not help the fact that she had married George Smythe; that was beside the point. He was in love with her and wanted her with him forever. They would remain in California and send for Fredericka. They would begin a new life and no one ever need know about Mary's previous poor choice of a husband, or that they were cousins. They were obviously passionately in love with one another, and no one would ever look down on them or scorn their decision. They, in fact, would be completely free to live, love, and raise the baby girl who had been named for him in the first place. They would have more children, and fit in comfortably with the new California lifestyle. Best of all, Mary would never need return to Maryland, never face George or any of his pampas critics.

Fred was confident that Mary felt the same, but was puzzled that she seemed to be in such turmoil. After all, why would she have accepted his mother's invitation to join them on this trip if she had not had the same scheme in mind? Surely, he surmised many weeks ago, that her intensions were parallel to his: that she would never to return to Maryland and would be his forever. The fact that they had never discussed the details *specifically* was for privacy and to preserve their plan.

The plan was perfectly clear in Fred's mind. The only confusing part was Mary's behavior of the last 48 hours. There was hesitancy on her part he had not anticipated, but he would just have to be patient. Perhaps he had underestimated the emotional ties between Mary and George, for whatever lame reason. Apparently, this was going to be a little more difficult for Mary than he thought. Soon enough, though, they would be in California and she would be entirely his.

What neither Fred nor Mary realized, however, was that when people want something desperately, they are remarkably good at self-deception.

Chapter 18

Letter Seven

Fri., March 13th
Nevada

We had a very good night's rest. It is so nice to have a compartment to yourself and to take your time to wash and dress. Fred and Max did not wait to eat breakfast with us. The meals are $1.00 a piece and we eat three a day. It would be better for us if we did not. The food is rich!

On our way from the dining car yesterday I felt so like helping with the dear little baby. The Papa looked so sad and forsaken. So, on getting back to our car, I told Fred. "Well," said he, "I'll take you back." So we got there just as the poor fellow was trying to change the little thing, so he let me finish. Told me all about the death of his wife on Friday in Denver, his future plans, and so forth. He was so thankful to me. Toward night, she got the colic. I was again able to help him; got some of Fred's brandy and made a little toddy which quieted her. He got off at 7 A.M. today.

We are not to stop over in Sacramento, but will send for our mail in case any has been sent there. Please direct next to San Buenaventura, Cal. care of Henry Branette, Esq.[21] Will write some now to Ma. The train is going quite fast and so it is rather difficult to write and you may have trouble to read.

I feel so thankful that we have been brought this far in safety, but ever since Mrs. Hamner[22] made such a beautiful prayer, I thought the

Lord would watch over us and the same God will protect my darling George and baby.

We reach San Francisco tomorrow noon where I will again write you. Will mail this sometime today. Give love to James and Natalie if she is still with you.

Fondly your wife,
Mamie

Have you recalled The Professor's name yet at Salt Lake?

Chapter 19

Somewhere in Nevada

Mary rested out of sheer exhaustion Thursday night. She awoke early in the morning, washed, and dressed for breakfast. She knew today would be a long day as it would be another full travel day on the train. Even brief stops helped break up the trip, but today few were scheduled, as this was a very remote part of the west. Today there would be limited reason for a reclusive stay in her sleeper; today she would undoubtedly face Fred.

She was pleasantly surprised when she arrived at breakfast to find that Aunt Emily was waiting alone. Fred and Max, it seemed, would not be joining them for breakfast. Mary knew then that Fred, too, was feeling some measure of anxiety and was not ready to face her this morning.

Yes, this would be a long day.

Most of the morning passed quietly without chance encounter. It was just before lunch, while Mary was comfortably reading in the library car, that Fred appeared.

"Good morning, Mary," he said with a kind smile and that voice.

Mary's book slipped to her lap as she returned his smile and greeting.

"May I join you?" he asked formally.

"I suppose…yes. Yes, of course you can," she smiled and nodded affirmatively. She knew she simply had to get over this foolishness, and this was as good a time as any to start.

"Thank you," he said, taking the seat next to her on the tapestry covered davenport. "You're looking very well this morning. Feeling much better, are you?" he began with polite conversation.

Why on earth did I leave myself wide open for anyone to sit so close? With all these comfortable chairs, I pick the sofa...she thought to herself as he sat down next to her.

"Yes, I'm feeling much better, thank you. I slept well and am ready for whatever the day brings my way," she added. How odd of her to say that she thought to herself.

"Excellent! I'll be ready to reach San Francisco, won't you? Train travel is certainly deluxe, but it is getting a little old, don't you think?" Fred asked Mary.

With a slight chuckle, she heartily agreed. "Yes, especially when one's prone to 'altitude sickness' to begin with! Whoever heard of such a thing?"

They both laughed comfortably, and each relaxed a little.

"Hopefully, the return trip will be a little easier," Mary added lightly. Little did she realize the door that she had just opened.

"You don't have to think about that now. Hopefully, that will be far in the future." Fred answered.

"It seems now like we've planned an extended stay," offered Mary innocently, "but I expect the time will absolutely *fly* by! I bet we'll be headed east before we even realize it. Seems that's the way with excursions...months and months in the planning, then they're over before you know it."

He did not answer. He didn't know what to say.

Mary noticed his silence. "Haven't you found that to be the way...months in planning and then over too quickly?" she asked him.

"Mary," he hesitated. "Is this simply 'an excursion' to you?"

"Oh, of course not, Fred. I'm sorry to be insensitive. It is a special and precious time to spend with Aunt Emily...and with you, of course," she dared to add. "It's been so long since we've all had a good visit, and to be able to do so while seeing California is truly a special treat. That's what I meant," she concluded and was satisfied with her explanation.

"I see," he said, but he really didn't see at all. He could not believe what he was hearing. They hadn't reached California yet, and she was already talking about her 'return trip'. This can't be. "Mary, you can't be thinking of that now!" he said in a very insistent manner.

"What on earth...."

"Mary, you aren't thinking of going back!"

"Well," she snapped, "of course not right now! In May, as planned. Fred, what's wrong with you?" She was getting just a little bit irked.

"Mary, I have no intension of letting you go back. Ever. I love you."

"Oh, Fred! That's absolutely ridiculous! Don't be a goose!"

"Isn't that precisely *why* you came, Mary, so that we would be together?" Fred nearly gritted his teeth as he quietly inquired. He enunciated his words slowly and clearly to be sure there was no mistake.

For Mary, it was if she were hearing this for the first time. In fact, she was. She was stunned and did not know what to say. She was wrestling with her own overwhelming emotions, but she had not taken her thoughts so far as to entertain the possibility of not returning home. Clearly, that was exactly what Fred had in mind. How could she have missed his intentions? Or had she known them all along?

Chapter 20

Saturday, March 14

Mary was still weak and a little unsteady as Fred helped her alight from the train. Having spent the last several days in the confinement of the train, her first glimpses of San Francisco were welcome ones. The bustling station seemed a hub of activity as travelers, luggage, porters, and attendants whirled around her.

"Wait here," Fred said as he planted his mother and Mary on the first available bench.

"Max, bring a carriage. I'll see that the porter offloads all our trunks. I'd rather double-check now than run the risk of coming up short once we reach the hotel."

Both men set off in opposite directions, each with their own mission in mind.

"*California!* Mary! California! I did expect it to be bright and sunny though, didn't you, dear? Seems a bit dreary and dismal to me. Maybe it's just the day. *San Francisco!* Can you imagine? We're in San Francisco! Breathe deeply, dear, just as the doctor ordered. Sloooow…deeeeep…breeeaaaths." Aunt Emily demonstrated as she spoke, standing straight as a soldier and filling her ample lungs with air.

Mary couldn't help but mimic what Aunt Emily was doing, and she smiled at herself.

"I'm fine, Aunt Emily. Really, I am. I admit it is good not to be in motion, though." She slowly nodded affirmatively as she spoke.

The two women sat silently watching the myriad of people coming and going throughout the station. Max promptly secured a carriage and, once Fred pronounced all luggage accounted for and being delivered directly to the hotel, the tourists began to make their way to their suites at the opulent Palace Hotel.

Mary slowly opened her eyes and batted her thick lashes a few times. She tried to focus, but regardless of her efforts, the figure over her was a blur.

"My darling, how are you?"

She could be blind as a bat and would still know the voice that melted her heart. Fred hovered near her, and gently stroked her tussled hair.

She blinked, and tried to focus again.

"What happened?" she murmured. Her head had a dull ache, and she reached for her temple.

Fred took her hand and kissed the back of it. "My darling," he sighed. "You fell, dear, but the doctor says you'll be fine. I won't let anything happen to you, my love. Just rest; I'll be right here."

"Where am I?"

"In your suite at the Palace Hotel. Do you remember that we are in San Francisco?"

"Yes," she answered tentatively. "The train...."

"Yes, the train. You are still weak from altitude illness and that, combined with the motion of the train, well, you just lost your balance. You collapsed when you got up from the bench, and I caught you just as you went down. The doctor says this could have been very serious, but fortunately, I was there to break your fall. You just need to rest...and take it slowly. I won't leave your side, Mary."

Mary sighed and sat up. Woozy, but as determined as ever, she reminded Fred that she hadn't come all this way to nap. In fact, she was famished and would really like to have some lunch. She threw the coverlet aside and swung her legs over the side of the bed. Her toes felt the floor for her little shoes.

"Well, then...ah...I guess that would be alright, but I won't leave you alone, Mary. I insist on staying with you," Fred said as he assisted her into her comfortable shoes.

"Fine, Fred," she snapped, "and I want to see the city! I've been cooped up in that train for days, and I want to go outside."

He knew from her tone that there would be no arguing with her, and he also knew it would not be the time for any further serious discussion regarding their future. That would have to wait for another time.

Chapter 21

The weather in San Francisco was even drearier on the second day than it had been on the group's first day in town. The two women did venture out to church, as was the habit of Aunt Emily. Regardless of where in the world she was, Sunday morning worship was always a priority. Mary knew from growing up in her household that she was expected to go, and never understood why the same was not expected of Aunt Emily's sons. This day, however, she was glad that Fred would not be joining them.

This Sunday morning Mary earnestly felt the need to be in church and to gain strength, or faith, or courage, or something; she wasn't sure what. She didn't consider herself to be a particularly religious person; however, she did consider her faith to be an important part of her life. She had "gone forward" one August when she was 14 at a church camp meeting that Aunt Emily had taken her to, but never felt any different and was never sure that anything spiritual had really happened. She knew she could pray and call on the Lord any time, and this was certainly one of those times. Without a doubt, this was one of those times.

The Presbyterian church that the concierge suggested was just a short carriage ride from the hotel. On the way back from the thought-provoking service, the women shared their carriage with another lady, and it was then that Mary met Mrs. Jennifer Heron. Mrs. Heron was a joyful woman, slightly younger than Mary and every bit as attractive. They had greeted each other in passing on the train, and both were staying in suites at the Palace Hotel. Now they finally had a few minutes to introduce themselves while returning from church.

"Will you meet me in the grand foyer for tea this afternoon, say 1:30?" Mrs. Heron cheerfully invited the two women.

"How kind of you, Mrs. Heron, but I think I'll pass," replied Aunt Emily quickly. "You two young ladies enjoy your visit and get to know one another. I hear the funeral procession for Senator Hearst is to assemble and I don't want to miss that! Rumor has it that there are an extraordinary number of dignitaries staying at our hotel, and I want to see what I can see!"

The young women looked at each other and both smiled at the thought of such entertainment, and agreed on 1:30 in the Tea Room of the Grand Foyer.

"You and your husband make such a handsome couple." Mrs. Heron began innocently enough as she added honey to her tea. "Where are you and Mr. Smythe from?"

Mary felt unusually at ease in the presence of this woman whom she had just met, but this would be awkward at best. She quickly realized her best reply was to be matter-of-fact and honest.

"I'm traveling with my aunt and cousin," Mary said as calmly as she could as she over-stirred her tea.

"Pardon me for my error. I just assumed…," Mrs. Heron trailed off.

"That's quite alright," Mary assured her, and offered no more information. She 'assumed' that most people 'assumed'. Perhaps they could avoid the subject entirely. "And where are you from?"

"Virginia, near Fredericksburg." Mrs. Heron answered proudly. "Do you know Virginia, or the eastern part of the country at all?"

"Oh my goodness! I'm from Maryland! Well, home is New Jersey, but I live in Maryland," remarked Mary. "How funny that we've met so far from home!"

The two women chatted casually and laughed over tea and delightful almond cookies for nearly an hour and a half before Fred appeared. It was so good to laugh, Mary thought to herself, but the arrival of Fred brought a halt to that gaiety.

"I'm so sorry to interrupt, Mary, dear, but I really do need to talk with you. Can you tell me when would good time for us to chat?" Fred cornered her, and she knew it. He knew she wouldn't snap at him or refuse him flatly in front of her new friend.

"Oh, I really do want to write some notes this afternoon," interjected Mrs. Heron. "Please excuse me. We've had a *lovely* visit, and we'll visit again soon, alright?"

"Oh no, no, you don't need to leave, Jennifer! Please stay." Mrs. Heron had no idea how much Mary meant it, but she politely refused.

"Thank you, no. We'll visit again very soon. Thank you for joining me, Mary! Good bye for now!" With that, Mrs. Heron took her leave, and both women knew they would indeed visit again.

Mary stared up at Fred, and instantly she knew that he meant business. She also knew there wasn't enough tea in China to calm the sudden flurry of butterflies in her stomach.

"Shall we walk?" Fred said as he leaned over to Mary, placed his hand under her elbow, and assisted her up from her comfortable chair. It was not a question, it was a statement, and Mary knew that they *were* going to take a walk.

"You missed an excellent sermon this morning, Fred. The message was on '…the foundation of God being a sure one, and the Lord knows those who are His, and of being a vessel of honor'." Mary stopped short of telling him the part about '…fleeing youthful lusts and following the Lord with a pure heart'.

"We're not talking about church, Mary. We need to talk about us." Fred continued without giving Mary and opportunity to interrupt. "I want to make my intentions perfectly clear, for apparently there has been a misunderstanding." He took a deep breath and added, "Mary, I have no intention of allowing you to return to Maryland. You are the love of my life, and your place is with me."

Mary just bristled at the familiar words. Why is it that the men in her life are so confident that they know where 'her place is' and that 'her place' is with them?

"I'm a married woman, Fred, and that's the end of that."

"It's not that simple, Mary. People make mistakes, and mistakes can be corrected. I know you *thought* you were in love with George, but nothing good will ever come of it." His tone softened and he stopped and turned to Mary. He took her hand in his and led her to be seated next to him on one of the beautiful, moss green imported European sofas under the Grand Dome of the Palace. "I knew when I held you in my arms the other evening that you are as much in love with me as I am with you. You can't deny it, Mary. I know it. I *felt* it. I want you here with me."

Mary knew he was right, at least the part about her being in love with him. It was true; he had felt it, and so had she.

Chapter 22

Letter Eight

Palace Hotel[23]
San Francisco, Cal.
Sunday Afternoon, Mar. 15th, 1891

My dear George,

We arrived yesterday about 1:00 p.m. After lunch and a wash, Fred and I went for a walk. The street was crowded and it struck us the women dressed rather loud, but I suppose we did not see the best people. The City Hall we passed; it is not yet finished and has cost $4,000,000. Calla lilies are just nothing! You see them growing in great numbers, even sticking through the fence! You can buy great bunches of violets for 10 cents!

This morning Aunt Emily and I went to church (Presbyterian) near here and heard a gentleman from Portland Oregon—Rev. Thomas Boyd. His sermon I enjoyed very much! It was from 2 Timothy, 2nd Chapter, first of 19th verse. "Nevertheless the foundation of God standeth sure." Really, the sermons I've been hearing lately have been treats!

It commenced to sprinkle and has proved a rainy afternoon. After lunch, we watched the departure from court-way of the Washington party for Sen. Hearst's[24] funeral. The complete list of pallbearers met here in Parlor A. Senator Faulkner is in the party. On our way up in elevator, I heard one gentleman say that he had not seen Senator Faulkner since they graduated at the University of Virginia in [18]'67.

81

He was going to see if he would know him. There were several very rich men on our train coming here. One was E. R. Rose the great horse-raiser. He makes thousands of dollars out of some of them! Then there was another old gentleman named Carr worth one or two million! There are plenty of men who can play Uncle to such as Mrs. Oster[25], and maybe such women ought not to be blamed so terribly! They do not feel they are robbing other women (in money), and then they may not have had loving mothers or faithful husbands to keep them true. They see all that wealth can give.

Did I tell you about the sacks upon sacks of silver ore that we saw going to the smelters while we were passing through Nevada, and the many Indians? As we drew nearer here we commenced to see the Chinese. There was a Chinese woman with her baby in the smoker (car). It was much cleaner and cuter-looking than the Indian ones who were brought to the trains on the mother's back and you were expected to pay for seeing it!

Our train passed through Benicia Arsenal where Mark was stationed. Just beyond that, at a place called Pt. Costa, the train runs on an immense ferry-boat[26]. One gentleman said it was the largest in the world! Certainly it was much larger than the B & O one at Cedar Point!

Fred took me on top of the boat, so I had quite a good view of Sacramento River. When you reach Oakland, you leave train to go on another large ferryboat; upper and lower decks like they are to have at Jersey City, and cross San Francisco Bay and are landed right at the dock. Tomorrow we will visit The Presidio[27]. I wish Major Gordon was still there. I have written to him; I do not think we can visit him. I think Aunt Emily was rather inclined to, but I have talked it over with Fred. We think it most too much of an extra trip for her just for one visit. It would be fully 1,000 miles there and back. He wrote me if we could not plan to come, he would meet us at Los Angeles, but I doubt if he would take that trouble and expense. However, I'll let them know, otherwise they might think I did not wish to meet them, and, to tell you the truth, I don't care much about it. But, he has been very kind in sending timetables from time to time. We leave here about Thursday for Monterey By The Sea; return on 23rd and 25th in Los Angeles at "The Nadeau".

PALACE
HOTEL

SAN CALIFORNIA FRANCISCO

·MENU·

Dinner,

Sunday March 15, 1891.

MENU

Soup
California Oysters on Shell
Printanier Royal — Cream of Barley

Fish
Fillet of Sole, Normande
Sardines, Mustard Sauce
Pommes Dauphine

Boiled
Leg of Mutton, Mashed Turinps
Corned Beef and Cabbage
Beef Tongue, Madeira Sauce

Entrees
Noie of Beef Braise, with Celery
Hare Saute a la Chasseur
Veal Cutlet Breaded a la Milanaise
Fillet of Mutton a la Bretonne

Cold
Lamb   Veal
Ham   Beef Tongue
Roast Beef   Celery   Lobster Salad

Roast
Beef   Spring Lamb, Mint Sauce   Veal
Turkey, Cranberry Sauce

Vegetables
Spinach   Rice   Stewed Tomatoes
Asparagus   Mashed Potatoes
Beets   Baked Potatoes

Dessert
English Plum Pudding, Rhum Sauce
Peach Tartelette   Rhubarb Pie
Dartois aux Pommes   Tricornes aux Confiture
Madeleines de Commercy   Pound Cake

Ice Cream
Sorbets au Kirsch   Philadelphia Ice Cream
Raspberry Ice Cream   Pineapple Water Ice

Almonds   English Walnuts   Raisins
Fruit   COFFEE   Cheese

DINNER, 6 to 8 P. M.

Late Supper Served in Restaurant, from 8 to 11:30 P. M.

PLEASE REPORT ANY INATTENTION OR DELAY TO THE STEWARD.

AMUSEMENTS
ALCAZAR THEATRE—A Night off.
Performance Every Evening and Saturday Matinee

Chapter 23

Letter Nine

Monday afternoon, Mar 16th.

Have waited till Max should go to P.O. He has just returned and says there is none for me; only for Aunt Emily. So, that will be home news. Had one letter from there this A.M. So pleased to hear from Natalie; tell her, please.

We four have been out to the Cliff House[28] & Sutro Park. It is lovely, and how I longed for you! It looks right over the Ocean and it was fun to see all the seals out over the rocks!

Max is waiting, so I must close. Will write you about it.

Hastily,
M

Chapter 24

Letter Ten

Palace Hotel San Francisco, Cal.
Tuesday evening, March 17ᵗʰ, 1891

Dearest George,

So much crowds in that I forget if yesterday I told you that we went after breakfast through "Nob Hill" where the railroad and other magnates live! Stanford, Flood, and Mrs. Mark Hopkins! Oh! Such immense houses! They overlook the city. We went to Cliff House, which is at the Southern head of the Golden Gate; it over hangs the Ocean! It is fun to watch the seal or sea-lion playing in the water! Back on higher bluffs was a lovely place: Sutro Heights Mr. Sutro lets people walk through his grounds which are filled with tropical plants, statuary, and so forth. Today we visited China-town. 30,000 population. Such a place I never will be able to tell you half!! We went in one of their restaurants and had tea and so forth. Saw some of them eating with their chopsticks. Tomorrow night Fred is going to take me to one of their theatres. He has gone with a guide tonight to visit the opium & gambling dens. There was a funeral today and such a racket as they made to keep the devil away and threw out prayers, one of which I got.

It is late; will write tomorrow. Haven't heard from you since at Denver; had nice one from Natalie. Love to her & James, in which Aunt Emily joins.

Lovingly,
M

I think I may as well keep on and tell you about how we spent the afternoon for tomorrow there will be something else. Well, we went out to Golden Gate Park. It contains 1,013 acres and is three miles long. The view is beautiful of the Ocean, Bay, and distant mountains, also city. There is Conservatory, Deer Park, Gymnasium, and so forth.

Thursday we leave for Monterey, stay till Monday then back here, leave Tuesday for Los Angeles reaching there March 25th. Write me at San Bernardino care of Henry Branette, Esq.; I sent his address. The Los Angeles address is "The Nadeau", but I don't think we will stay long enough to write there, but do let me hear at Mr. Branette's. We leave word about mail and I hope to hear tomorrow.

Yours always

Chapter 25

Letter Eleven

San Francisco Mar 18ᵗʰ '91

My dear Geo,

Yours of 12ᵗʰ received this afternoon & it has made me feel very uneasy about the baby, for in all our letters they have said nothing to worry me, only that she was cutting more teeth & of course her bowels would be out of order as they have been with each one she has cut up to date. Dr. Andrews, who we all have much faith in, said that was nothing to be alarmed about. I hope you will go up & see her & no doubt you can get Ma to do as you think best. But I don't know as you had best to urge Natalie to stay against her will. Had one letter from Ma this afternoon & she spoke of her bowels, but said the Dr. said they need not worry. You know they had better be that way than constipated when cutting teeth. I trust Natalie is unnecessarily worried as she & Aunt Rachael were when we sent for Dr. Wells this winter. You know she loves her dearly & maybe hasn't been with teething children.

Haven't time to write of today's doing; will from Monterey where we go tomorrow. Phil Gibson is here calling; has been very kind. Splendid fellow. You would never know him. Fred is also writing home about the baby & her drinking water.

Will send to Sacramento for my letters; they haven't been forwarded. Aunt Emily and Fred wish to be remembered.

Hastily
M

Chapter 26

Her days had been full and exciting, in many ways. Sightseeing throughout San Francisco exposed Mary to everything from an even more opulent lifestyle than she was used to, to poverty such as she had never seen. A trip through Chinatown was quite a novelty and a great deal of fun, until it dawned on Mary that some people lived their entire lives with very few material possessions. Nob Hill, on the other hand, was much more to her liking, and it was there that Fred promised her the world. He was relentless in his quest, yet somehow they managed to enjoy several wonderful days in that bustling city. Tensions were slightly eased between the two of them, partly due to the fact that Aunt Emily and Max had been ever-present during the last few days.

On Tuesday evening, Fred went out with some gentlemen with whom he had recently made the acquaintance, and Aunt Emily took her meal in her suite. Mary dined in the main hotel dining room in the Palace Hotel with her new friend, Jennifer Heron.

It was while they were enjoying the fresh fruit cup that the women's conversation turned to the powerful sermon they both heard in church the previous Sunday.

"Yes, it was an *excellent* sermon," Mary agreed. "He was quite good...really left one thinking about what's of value."

"It is so important for us, as good Christian ladies," Jennifer added as she casually enjoyed a fresh chunk of pineapple, "to maintain every appearance of integrity. The world around us can be so vile and there are so many temptations at every turn. I really do struggle sometimes with efforts to maintain a pure heart, just as the pastor was talking about Sunday. Do you ever feel that way, Mary?"

Mary burst into tears, and Mrs. Heron's easy smile quickly turned to a look of horror. She had no idea what a difficult week it had been for Mary, emotionally, or how their innocent conversation had just hit the nail squarely on the head.

Once again, the old monogrammed hankie reappeared from Mary's evening bag and mopped more tears. During the course of the next several hours, and over much more tea, Mary poured her heart out to her new friend. Somehow, she instinctively knew that Mrs. Heron would never be judgmental or critical of her dilemma but would be a source of continual strength and encouragement as Mary struggled with her very divided heart.

Mary was horrified to learn that Fred had been to a gambling and opium den, but her insatiable curiosity quickly overwhelmed her disgust. She asked so many questions that even she thought she sounded just like Aunt Emily.

"What was it like inside? Was it dark and smoke-filled? Were there *women* in there? What were they wearing? Did they talk to you? Did you gamble in American or did you have to play in Chinese? Did you win? Oh, my...do tell me about *opium*! What's it like Fred? Did you *try* it?"

He could not contain his laughter at this elegant lady's barrage of questions and apparent thirst for knowledge of the seedier side.

"You are *so* comical, my dear! You want to maintain all appearances of a proper lady while all along you hunger for all that is new and different from what you're used to. You know there's more out there than your pampered life has exposed you to and you want it all. Your zest for life will *never* be satisfied living the role you've chosen for yourself, Mary," he concluded.

She had never heard that voice have such a sinister tone and his words affected her deeply.

"Here's what we'll do," Fred said with a charming smirk. "I'll take you to the Chinese Theatre and you can see for yourself. It won't be the same as the men's club, but it's the best I can offer you, my dear."

Mary was so excited at the prospect that she jumped up and hugged him as hard as she could. And, once again, he just held her close.

On Thursday, the travelers left San Francisco and moved to their next destination: Monterey. The lovely Hotel Del Monte would be their base for the next several days, and the incredible beauty of the area would provide a natural and very romantic backdrop for Fred to continue to woo Mary.

Chapter 27

Letter Twelve

Hotel Del Monte[29]
Monterey, Cal.
March 20, 1891

Dearest Geo,

All I ask for this minute is the power to half tell you of this Heavenly place. It seems to me that when we awake in Heaven we shall feel something as I do now! Oh, darling, it is so beautiful! Aunt Emily and Fred say there is nothing in Europe to compare to it! I think I shall never again be quite happy till you, Ma, & Fredericka have beheld it!

We reached here 1 PM yesterday and after a delicious lunch Fred, Max, & I started for a walk and at every turn new beauties dawned! There is also every thing to make children happy. Fred says our girlie must be brought here some day. We came to a "maze." Well, we started in and I thought we never would find our way out! Finally we saw two ladies laughing as heartily as ourselves and on asking them if they expected to get out they said they had traced their way in so we followed their track out, or we might have been there yet! Mrs. Hammond, I suppose has seen many of them in the gardens of Europe. This morning we got separated from Fred so Max and I walked to the Ocean and saw parts of whales. The bones were bleached as white as this paper, and then we walked to Monterey. You see the hotel grounds are about a mile from village. After lunch we all had a grand drive. Saw several old Spanish buildings, an old Monastery in ruins, the buildings where the 1ˢᵗ legislature of California was held, then to a place called Pacific Grove. They call it their Chautauqua (don't laugh at that spelling) of the West. Some pretty cottages & large hotel run by same company as this. We had thought to leave tomorrow and spend Sunday at Santa Cruz. Phil Gibson was to come down tomorrow eve but we are so in love with this place we wish to stay so Fred wrote Phil & invited him to spend Sun. with us. Phil is a splendid fellow. Fred is very much taken with him; says he hasn't met anyone in a long time he liked so well. Now he wants to go to Fort H_, but I don't. Indeed anything that will keep any longer away does not please me.

I wonder if you will spend Easter with our child. I enclose a little Easter card for Mrs. A. I ought to send one to Natalie, but I can't get any here.

Have bought many little things for different ones. Give love to James. Is he with you or boarding with Mrs. Barr?

I think it a very good idea to do with the Beach payment as you propose.

Our rooms are three connecting; beautiful! Through Phil Gibson we met a niece of Sharon[30] (very rich) and she wrote to her friends in Santa Cruz to call, but they are very rich & gay and I know Aunt Emily & I would not enjoy it. Too much wine, but it was good in her.

Your own,
Mamie

Chapter 28

Letter Thirteen

Hotel Del Monte
Monterey, Cal.
Palm Sunday, March 22, 1891

My dear Husband

This is a beautiful Sun. but the wind blows. Fred and I took a walk on the beach before lunch. Phil Gibson did not come and we were all disappointed. Aunt Emily too has taken a great fancy to him. Phil says she reminds him so much of Ma. Yesterday aft Aunt Emily, Max, and I took an 18-mile drive on a macadamized road through a forest of oaks & pines through which you catch glimpses of the Pacific. Soon we came to the far-famed cypress. There is no other place in the world that it grows. There is something in Lebanon like it but it is not the same. They are low & spreading, and seem to cling for dear life to the rocks. The driver said some of them were supposed to be 1000 yrs old. Then we came to Seal Rock. Clinging to the sides & peak were thousands of seals. There are more seals here than at any other point on the coast. Then you leave the shore & drive into more pines and oh such beautiful spots! I never shall forget that ride. Fred and a Mr. Wolly took it in the morning. We went through a settlement of Chinamen, they were drying fish & this seemed to draw the gulls for there was about a thousand on the ground. We are not the only ones charmed with the place for people from all over say it is the most beautiful place they ever saw. Last night

I dreamed you had exchanged our house for a place on Capitol Hill, bathroom & c. Expect to find letters on returning to San Francisco tomorrow; I pray constantly that our baby girl is better. Give love to James & remember wherever I am my heart is with you.

M

Chapter 29

Letter Fourteen

Hotel Del Monte
Monterey, Cal.

I keep forgetting to tell you that when we went through San Jose I could see the Lick Observatory. The dome was shining in the sun.

I have not said any thing about your plans for I know you would rather do your own planning but forgive me this once if I simply suggest that it would be so much better & easier for you, I should think, if you would consent to board. I mean take your meals with Mrs. Welsh or with the lady Mrs. White boards with. It would not cost you much more & would be so much nicer for you. Natalie has excellent reasons for not remaining & you can't blame her. Now don't think I want to plan for you. Only I can't help feel so.

Your loving wife Mamie

Hope to hear tomorrow at San Francisco

Chapter 30

The time spent in Monterey had been blissful, romantic, and utterly confusing. It was a time of intimate conversations and deep soul-searching, and a time that would, ultimately, change Mary forever. Visits to what were fast becoming 'tourist sites' with Aunt Emily and Max were offset by quiet walks near pristine coves and on isolated beaches alone with Fred. The stunning scenery of Monterey's dramatic coastline heightened all her emotions and the thundering of the waves echoed the pounding of her heart and the crashing of her thoughts.

The sermon on Palm Sunday, once again, Mary concluded, was directed specifically at her. The Pastor preached on having a relationship with the One True and Living God rather than practicing a hollow and lifeless religion. He explained that there must be a "change of heart; a change from inside out" that resulted in a lifestyle of holiness and obedience, and a surrendering of one's own will in favor of the Lord's will for us. He ended his powerful message with Jesus' words in John 14:6: "I am the Way, the Truth, and the Life; no one comes to the Father but through Me."

It was almost as if she was hearing it for the first time. Although Mary had heard the truth of God's Word throughout the years, somehow the situation she found herself in caused her to reevaluate her need for Divine direction and guidance, and peaked her spiritual thirst. The majestic seaside environment caused her to recall from somewhere in her past, the scripture verse about the person who lacks wisdom as being "…unstable…and driven and tossed by the sea."[31]

"Lacking wisdom," "unstable," and "tossed" were all accurate descriptions of the ways in which Mary was feeling. Each hour of each day seemed to bring her more confusion rather than clarity, and over the course of the next several weeks, she would find herself repeatedly calling on the Lord for His help. It was only now that she was even able to begin to define some of her thoughts, and they scared her terribly. She was realizing that she was in love with two men, one of whom was her husband and the other was not.

Fred was so persuasive and charming. He was gentle and kind and truly did promise her the world. Although they both suspected their genuine love for one another quite early on, it was only by being separated that their feelings for each other were solidified. Fred never thought that Mary would, in fact, marry George Smythe, but she had. Not only had they wed, but also they had moved away from the New Jersey homestead to Maryland, and Fred was heartbroken. She did not even live close enough for the cousins to visit, much less for him to be able to keep watch over the love of his life. Shortly after her marriage, Fred moved to Hays, Kansas, in an attempt to remove himself as far from the known world as he could. Now, the two were reunited, together for at least eight romantic weeks, and hopefully, Fred had decided, forever.

Mary was realizing that there was something very exciting about being 3,000 miles from home and in places where no one knows who you are. She found it enticing and quite easy to enjoy the freedom afforded her by her unfamiliar surroundings and Fred's extremely lavish spending. She had not anticipated that this would be anything more than a simple vacation with Aunt Emily, and a time to visit with Fred. She had seriously underestimated the lure and the romance of the fact that she was completely unknown: no one knew her marital status or her responsibilities as a wife and mother. There were no expectations, and, for that matter, no rules to follow other than what she determined to be right at any given moment. There was something tantalizing about knowing that perfect strangers thought she and Fred to be a "charming couple."

Mary was precariously close to crossing a line, which once crossed, she would never fully return. It was a time of serious personal reflection such as Mary had never known before, and it wore her down. Nevertheless, she decided, at least for the time being, to enjoy all that was before her. There was so much that was beautiful and exciting, and the fact that she had an adoring and handsome escort to help her experience it was, well, all the better.

Chapter 31

Letter Fifteen

Hotel Nadeau[32]
Los Angeles, Cal
March 25, 1891

Darling. We arrived at 4 PM (1 hr late) left San Francisco yesterday at 4. The road did not run through such a lovely valley as Monterey. This morning we passed over a wonderful piece of work called the "Loop" were the road crosses & recrosses. It was 3,792 ft long. 352 miles from San Francisco. After that we went through Majovie Desert. Nothing grew there but the yucca palm. Before reaching here we passed through a tunnel—took 5 minutes. I have not been out and around, but I'm not much struck with Los Angeles. Fred doesn't like hotel although we have best rooms, bath & c. each have a room. Aunt Emily was tired and has gone to bed. Fred & Max are out. Max has all we have but he does not eat at same table. Fred said he never had to correct but one thing in his table manners. Sometimes he would put his knife in his mouth. I like him so much.

Telegram from Col. Gordon came for me after we had left for Monterey last week. I didn't get it till yesterday. Fred thought it should be answered and I didn't. I'll tell you why when I come home although I guess you will laugh at me. I've lots to tell you! The women out here are queer some of them and you'll think so too.

These little poker slips I took from two papers a gentleman gave me last night. Who does that wife remind you of? See how they got my name in this last time and I wonder if Col. & Mrs. Yates are the parents of young Yates. His father was in the Army. I am rather tired myself and my light shines into Aunt Emily's room and it may keep her awake so I'll bid you good night. Indeed dear I wish for you every day and wish I could say good night in person. Don't forget the Camphor in my furs. Will tell you of here after I've seen it.

Yours faithfully
M

San Buenaventura

Chapter 32

Letter Sixteen

Hotel Nadeau
Los Angeles, Cal.
Mar 27th, 1891
Good Friday evening

My dear Husband,

A letter from you this morn written on 18th made me happy, before we started out on our sightseeing and our baby's postal enclosed. How I have wished for you today; you would have so enjoyed it. But first I must tell you how yesterday was spent. After breakfast we took a cable car way out to one end of the city. We saw such pretty homes and lovely lawns; they build very nice homes for $1500 or so. "Old Baldy"[33] we saw plainly covered with snow. Then we went out to other end of city through the orange groves. After lunch Aunt Emily went to hear a converted Jewish, while Fred, Max, and I out to a concert at Eastlake Park. The park is only 2 years old so we didn't find much. Consequently, we left soon and went to Ever Green Cemetery. One lot was so odd! There was a handsome granite monument and all over the ground chips of granite were strewn. Not a speck of ground was left for even a blade of grass to come through. There was one fine vault and it was spoiled by having in it a cane-seat rocker and a stand & c. We could see through the glass door. In the evening Fred and I took a walk. This morn he and I went to an old Mexican Mission Church. Being Good Friday, there was service. All seemed to be Mexicans. At 11 a.m.

we four left for Arcadia: 16 miles, where is the great Ranch of "Lucky" Baldwin[34]*. It contains 50,000 acres! After a lovely lunch at a hotel there, we took a carriage and went all over it, through the great groves of oranges (of which we could pick all we wished). We saw groves of figs, English walnuts, apricots and vineyards; oh so large! Then we went to his winery. Why, one thing held 4,000 gallons and I don't know how many there were of those! Different year's make. We were offered some, but you know Aunt Emily and I never indulge when well. From there we went to the Stables. We saw "Emperor of Norfolk" which in 2 seasons won $87,000. He has several other celebrated ones. One tiny colt, 12 hours out, was worth $5,000. Just to think, he was offered $3,000,000 for 100 acres! We saw several artesian wells. They go down about 200 ft. Went through lemon groves also. I never expect to see such a place again. After seeing his home (when here, for you know he lives in San Francisco) which, by the way, had the cutest log hut on the lawn and which would be lovely for our Freddie's*[35] *play house. We drove to the Old San Gabriel Mission. Again found services. I wish I could tell you how old & quaint it is. Maybe your Raymond Book tells.*

From every place nearly today we could see the Hotel Raymond. Tomorrow we go over there.

I can't remember about Mr. McGuire.

Good night dear. I'm too tired to write more.

Lovingly

M

Ventura next

Written on the back of the Hotel Nadeau Wine List

P.S.
Did not know till today you would rather I direct to Hyattsville[36].
Mr. Lanham (Fred's friend) has just called. He is a Yale graduate and
practices law here. Fred told me something about him which makes me
admire him very much. I'll tell you sometime. I was just telling Aunt
Emily she ought to have brought some of her unmarried nieces for we
meet so many single gentlemen. You know Mr. Branette is a bachelor
also. He seems just delighted to think we are to visit him and writes the
nicest letters when he remails our. Aunt Emily says she knows Fred
would not have any of the others unless it was Florence Lyton[37]. Yes,
Ventura is right but the people like San Buenaventura best. Still write
there. We will be there a week from Tuesday.

Yours always,

Chapter 33

Letter Seventeen

Hotel Nadeau
Los Angeles, Cal.
Mar 29th, 1891 Easter Morn

My dear Husband

Oh, what a beautiful Easter. The sun and everything seems to say, "The Lord is risen indeed!" All the churches seem to be making preparations. At one of the Methodist ones, 2,500 calla lilies are to be used. Methodist Churches here, till, as Fred says, "You can't rest." Will tell you of yesterday and later I will tell you how we spend this day. In the morning Fred, Max, and I went to see the Fruit Exhibit. One pear weighed 32 oz. and an orange 29 oz.! There was a sweet potato that I tried to remember it weighed, for it was immense. After lunch we three took train for Pasadena (9 miles). Then Fred had a carriage and we saw the place and the Hotel Raymond. One of the gardens had a Century plant in bloom and bananas growing. Then we had pointed out about the place where John Brown's sons lived. Pasadena is where Miss Laura Neuhaus' cousins lives, but I hadn't time to call, but may tomorrow as we want Aunt Emily to see this lovely spot. We went to St. Paul's Episcopal Church where one of Fred's schoolmates is a vestryman. It was very much crowded, but Rector Bugbee was so kind to us. It was beautifully trimmed. The Masons, with a good band, have just marched by. They have a service in the Simpson Methodist Church.

When we came in, I found your letters of the 10th and 20th and one from home. You see I don't always get them in order. That accounts for not answering your questions sometimes. They follow us from place to place. I think one of your Denver ones I may have lost, and the papers, but we have been quite fortunate not to miss more. I see Sect P[38]. is expected. I think Col. Gordon would have been here. In one of the personals of our party, Fred is spoken of as "...wealthy & c." He certainly spends money so!

How would it do if you and James don't want to board to get Lulie[39], and Natalie could train her in a little before she leaves?

Aunt Emily sends love and I do too with kisses added.

Mame

Chapter 34

Letter Eighteen

The Stewart
San Bernardino, Cal.
Mar. 31, 1891

My dear Geo

We arrived here at 2:25 p.m. yesterday. Stopped in Pasadena again and took another delightful drive, and Fred and I called on Dr. Reynolds.[40] *He was very kind and seemed much pleased to hear news from Miss Lizzie and all. He has the quaintest home. A little vine-covered cottage and out back is a tent in which he say he lives all the year. It was as artistic as you can imagine, and we were both mere charmed and Fred got some new ideas. When we reached here Aunt Emily and I took a rest, and then carriage to see an old lady friend of Grandmother Remsley's. She came out last year to visit. Her two sons, live on their Ranch two miles out. She was full of fun! Ma and Uncle James (Josh B. Remsley's father) used to go to school with him. Her sons are devoted to her, especially her unmarried one.*

I want to write Natalie but don't know where she is so will enclose it in this and you can forward. When we reach Hotel Del Coronado, I will have letters as Mr. Branette will forward. We reach there Fri. night. That day we will go over the line into Mexico! Aunt Emily and I will spend Thursday with a friend of Ma's on our way to San Diego.

Chapter 35

Letter Nineteen

Hotel Glenwood[41]
Riverside, Cal.
April 1, 1891

Dearest

Yesterday at noon we arrived here and after lunch we four took a drive all over. I will not write much of it, as by looking at your Raymond books you can read of the beautiful driveways with palms on each side of the way. It was for miles and handsome homes, several of which the driver took us into the grounds of, where we saw dates and so forth growing. We stopped at one place and bought oranges. It was run by three ladies from Canada with the add of one Chinaman. When one looks at the miles of orange groves, you wonder how they can all be used.

This morning Aunt Emily and I went out and bought some little things for those at home. Fred is real good; anything he thinks I want, he gets. Seeing so many lemons I said that makes me think of when a child, how I enjoyed a stick of candy in one. So after dinner, in he came with the lemons and 1 doz. sticks of candy. I said I should think the candied fruit would be very nice, not meaning I wished any, but yesterday he bought me a beautiful boxful. He, this afternoon, has gone to Redlands. Some say they think it is going to be a greater place for fruit than this.

It is two years today since Mamma[42] died. I am going to write to Natalie now, will you please forward as I do not know where she is. I see by papers there was a severe storm at Martinsburg.

Fondly
M

Chapter 36

Letter Twenty

Postmarked:
Tijuana, Mexico
Baja, California
Apr 3ʳᵈ

Dearest,

I am here. Where are you

Yours always & every where
Mamie

Chapter 37

Letter Twenty-One

Hotel Del Coronado[43]
April 4th, 1891

My dear Geo

    7:30 a.m. Apr. 2nd we left Riverside where I wrote you last. At 11 o'clock, we reached Arcadia where Mrs. Durand lives in a very nice cottage on the bluff overlooking the sea and a beautiful fertile valley. Opposite her is the San Diego Gun Club House. The keeper and his wife (Bryant, by name) are the only neighbors she has. They were so good to her when ill. Mrs. Durand says she remembers seeing you when she'd call to see Ma and you were visiting before we were married. Oh, if we could spend a few months in such a place we would be so happy! The beach is beautiful, then you look on the other side and there are the mountains with snow, and such gardens as they have! We had new peas, potatoes, and such for dinner. They took us through the Club House; it was furnished nicely and built on this plan: (there is a tiny sketch on the original letter) *"Catchee?"*

    At 8:20 p.m. Max and Fred met us at the San Diego depot. They had very nice rooms for us at the hotel and at 10:00 a.m. yesterday we four started for Tijuana, Mexico. We were joined by a San Francisco party who we met at Riverside. Such a nice family, a Mrs. Britton (a widow) and her only child; a splendid young lady and her niece and nephew and a Mr. & Mrs. Lander. Well, such fun as we had when we got there!

111

The stage took us to the Custom House where the Spanish official kindly stamped our handkerchiefs; I think he would have stamped us all over had we wished it! Then we went to the P.O. where I wrote you two or three lines. Hadn't time for more as I was afraid I'd get separated from the party for they had gone into a store to buy things. Then the droll darkey who rode on ahead and explained the points of interest and showed us the work of the recent flood. It was a sad sight. Going down, a gentleman who reminded me of you, dearest, was very kind to tell me things about places we passed. I enjoyed more the resemblance. On the return, we visited Sweet Water Dam. It holds 6,000,000,000 gals. 90 ft. high. We reached here about 4:00 p.m. The flags were still up for Sect. P. I forgot to say he followed us in 10 minutes Thursday night. Our rooms here are lovely over-looking the sea. It is the finest hotel I ever saw. I will mail you one of the books so you can see.

After breakfast today we went to the Museum. You can read about them. We went to the Ostrich Farm where we saw many of them. They are awfully hateful and when the keeper tried to make them run so he could show us where the best feathers come from, they made such a queer sound! He gave me a feather.

The hedges look so pretty out here. I hope ours will get a good start and look thrifty this summer like Mr. Anderson's. So many windmills here have vines covering the frame part. It is a wonder Mr. A. never had them on his as it adds greatly to the appearance.

I know the home folks were pleased at the Building Association interest. Has James put his in yet? When we have any to spare, that is a good place and should we ever have a chance to buy in town[44], we would be glad to have some toward it.

I so hoped to have letters on reaching here but I presume Mr. Branette thought there wasn't time enough to remail them. We may hear on reaching Los Angeles on Monday. We leave there Tuesday for Ventura. The people like their old name best: San Buenaventura. I've not heard from you dear since yours of March 20th. Do you wonder I long for a letter? No one knows how I want my husband, mother, and baby. The last we heard from Newark was the 20th. Remember me to

Mrs. Ungerford. Give love to Mrs. Hammond and James. I wonder if Mrs. Ralston (the elder) received the paper I sent. It had in it about the W—Press Assn. of Pacific Coast and I thought it might interest. When we leave here we will be on our return.

Fondly your own true wife,

The 2nd largest lighthouse in the world is near here.

(over)

On the reverse side of the original letter, Fred adds:

My dear George,
We are all having a good time and I hope you are having the same.
Sincerely,
F.D.

Chapter 38

Letter Twenty-Two

Hotel Del Coronado
Sunday, April 5, 1891

Aunt Emily and I are going to church. Have you been lately? I wish
you would some Sunday. Dr. Bailey[45] would be so pleased to see you.
Ask him about his daughter Miss Laura. I had a dream about her. It
was strange for I had not been thinking of her

This portion of the letter, which is written in ink, stops abruptly here.
The same sheet of paper is then turned sideways, and the following is
written in pencil:

In dining room. This room would please you as it is entirely arched
over with wood but I presume the book tells that. There is such a cranky
man & woman growling all the time about the waiter. I do so dislike it.
Wasn't it queer Aunt Emily should pray for Dr. Bailey when I had
just spoken in my letter and not out loud at all?

Chapter 39

Del Coronado Hotel, San Diego

"Tonight, Mary." Fred pulled her close and spoke softly as he repositioned a breeze-blown wayward lock from her face. "I've reserved the Presidential Suite for us."

"Fred…."

"Not a word; don't speak a word." He helped her steady herself and regain her footing on the narrow, sandy path to the beach. Wild grasses swayed in the warm and gentle breeze and added a natural melody to the exquisite shoreline scenery. "Not a word, my beloved."

Mary knew she needed to be silent, against her impulse, and think this through. They reached the open shoreline and walked the beach in silence.

"There is nothing that you or Fredericka will ever be lacking. You've seen the splendor of this land…you can't deny its beauty. I'm about to purchase the finest orange grove in all the County and you'll have the home the likes of which you've never even dreamed imaginable. We'll send for your Ma and the baby immediately…they'll be *here* with us before you're even scheduled to return to Maryland. This is a land of plenty, Mary, and I intend to capitalize on its riches, and I want you to share it all with me. I love you, Mary, and I want to fulfill…."

"George." She interrupted his litany of tempting words. "I love *George,*" she said in an anguished voice.

"You love *me!*" Fred insisted. "I know you do, Mary." He was confident of that. "And, in time you'll get over George," he added with an irritating shrug and a raise of his dark eyebrows.

"He would be devastated. He adores Fredericka so much."

"My point exactly: he doesn't adore *you*."

"Oh, he does!" snapped Mary. "Of course he loves *me*. And I love *him!*"

Fred tensed the left corner of his mouth in skepticism. "Are you trying to convince me or yourself, Mary?"

She thought quietly to herself as they walked on, stooping occasionally to sort through some unfamiliar beach treasure in the sand. The hem of her skirts were wet from the gentle waves, as were her tiny shoes, but she hadn't even noticed. When she spoke, she chose her words slowly and carefully.

"Some things are more important."

"And what could possibly be more important than our love? Fred was quick to defend his position. "I suppose the chatter of the old ladies in Hyattsville is "important", and the talk around George's Washington Gentlemen's Clubs would be "important". You can't worry about those kinds of things, Mary. You'll be far removed and it won't matter. It won't matter one bit."

There was that sarcasm that she so dearly hated.

"No, that's not what I had in mind." She stopped short of completing her thought, and they walked on, this time taking a slighter higher path to avoid the wet sand.

"Answer me, Mary. What's more important than our love, and being together for the rest of our lives? What's more important than raising Fredericka in luxury and giving her everything her little heart desires? What's more important than our happiness and having everything we want?"

Mary stopped and looked out to sea. She had no idea how long she stood there, recalling the joys of the past few weeks mingled with remembrance of the frustration under which she left home. '...driven and tossed by the waves', she recalled somewhere in the mix of jumbled thoughts. She finally turned to Fred, looked him squarely in those dangerously enticing eyes, and stated flatly, "A clear conscience."

Chapter 40

Letter Twenty-Three

Hotel Nadeau
April 6, 1891

My dear Geo

As I wrote yesterday from Coronado, I thought only to send you a postal from here, but I must have just a few minutes with my dear, far away husband. I feel just a little nearer to you than I did yesterday. You see, by heading we have returned here, so now are on our homeward way. Tomorrow we leave for Mr. Branette's.

Where I shall find your Easter letter, for Natalie says you have written one?

From there we go to the valley; that takes us three or four days, then to Salt Lake where you can next write. I don't know which hotel we will be at as yet, so just direct to General Delivery and we will call for them.

Chapter 41

Mary sat quietly in the federal blue brocade rocker, flexing her left foot only occasionally to engage the rocker just a little at a time. She was deep in thought and reflecting on the day, and was, of course, sipping hot tea. Her delicate hands wrapped around the fine porcelain teacup and the warmth comforted her. She had foregone dinner; a silver tray with assorted fresh fruit, cheese and various crackers was brought to her room as requested. It was good to be alone in the comfort and quiet of her suite.

She knew she was making the right decisions, but her heart was in agony. How could this have happened to her, she pondered over and over and over? How is it that she could find herself in love with someone other than her husband, and question her devotion to the man to whom she was married? After all, she didn't have a wandering heart and truly did love George. As a Christian woman, she knew better, for heaven's sake, and she was brought up with clear values and good morals. She was raised in the church and knew right from wrong, but she finally concluded, being in church didn't guarantee immunity from temptation. What on earth had derailed her to the point where she would even entertain the thoughts that she had? Worse yet, she had to admit to herself that she had thoroughly enjoyed those thoughts, and tears streamed down her cheeks.

Mary sorted through her trunks to find the old worn leather Bible Ma had given her many years ago. She didn't read it on a regular basis, but she never traveled without it. Somewhere buried in the enormous heap of clothing, accessories, jewelry, and gifts she'd purchased along the way, she knew she had to find it and just read. Anything. Psalms or

Proverbs would provide comfort and wisdom; she knew that much. Beyond that, she didn't know.

The young woman read, and prayed, and talked to the Lord, as she had not done in a very long time. Late into the night, she poured out the pain in her heart and longed for peace in her soul. She had been in turmoil over one thing or another for so long…and felt so weary.

When Mary read the verse "…but as for me, my feet were almost gone; my steps had well nigh slipped…."[46] she blatantly saw herself. She recognized that *her* feet had nearly stumbled. She knew the imaginations of her heart had been running riot. She didn't recall ever before reading the part about if you *know* what is the good and right thing to do, and you *chose* not do it, you have sinned."[47] Throughout the night, Mary thought hard about character qualities such as faithfulness and commitment, integrity and honor, and reaffirmed in her own jumbled mind that *these* were the things of true value. She determined that night to stay the course and trust God with all her heart, and not to lean on her own understanding.[48] There was so very much, she didn't understand, but He promised to direct her steps and she needed to place her trust firmly in Him and not in what she could see enticingly before her. Certainly, she could trust Him over what her emotions had been telling her.

She asked the Lord to forgive her for her past indiscretions; no, they were *sins* and she was, for the first time, truthful with herself about that much at least. She recognized, too, that what she liked to call her 'present situation' was more than just treading on thin ice. It was only by God's grace and His intervention that she had been kept from making a terrible mistake.

There was a flicker of joy when she realized God's protection in her life, and those thoughts brought just the hint of a smile to her drained face. She silently thanked the Lord for being with her, and asked Him to take control of her life. She thanked Him for His saving grace.

Mary knew she had come too close to choosing to stay with Fred and sending for the baby. The attractive lure of lavish riches, words of endless adoration, and the promise of a life of ease was almost overwhelming. She came too close to walking away from the man she married. In the quiet of her heart, late that night at the Del, Mary reaffirmed to herself and her Lord that she loved the man she had married, and she wanted to be with George forever. Mary had finally resolved that integrity and obedience to the Lord's direction are more enduring than anything the world would offer her. And, beyond that, her reward would be eternal.

Chapter 42

Letter Twenty-Four

Hotel Nadeau
April 7, 1891

Was too sleepy to write much last night. Aunt Emily and I went out to visit the Chinese Kindergarten this morning—found it closed, but was in Chinatown where Aunt Emily bought some little bags for her Sunday School Class.

You were quite safe in betting with May D. that if I was unmarried, and wanted to be, I think I would come here. It is a long way for her to come and will be hard I imagine for her to leave her family.

Had a letter dated 31ˢᵗ from Natalie last night. How our little darling seems to grow into everyone's love. I was quite amused at Natalie not liking Ike[49] much! You have to learn his ways first.

Had a long letter from Col. Gordon; he is much disappointed at not seeing us.

Right after lunch we start for Ventura. I must close now with love to Natalie, James and a great deal for your dear self.

As ever and forever your
M

Very sorry to hear of Dr. Richmond's illness.

Chapter 43

Letter Twenty-Five

Hotel Del Coronado
"Sea View"
Ventura April 8, 1891

Have written you a postal dearest today, and now I will take more time, and answer some of your dear, interesting letters. You have written so faithfully, and I assure you, darling, every word has been appreciated. Thanks especially for your Easter one. It was so lovely and long and although it contained news I would rather not have heard, still it does not make me any more uneasy about Fredericka for I know they are taking as good care of her as they can and if God saw best to take my darling, why my love could not keep her any more than did Mr. and Mrs. Ungerford with the constant and never ceasing care of Dr. Richmond. I do hope he will get well and the others of the family. How much sickness there is in Hyattsville! What did Minnie's and Aunt Rachael's children die of? I suppose Mrs. Hammond rather expected her brother's death. You and James must take the very best care of yourselves and if Natalie is with you, see that she doesn't get one of her colds if possible. Thanks for Mrs. Prather's, and how sweet of her to be thankful and to show it. Do answer it for I think she feels it when you don't and she is too sweet and true to you to even seem to neglect her. I should imagine that her niece might have grown into a very pretty young lady for I saw here when a little girl at Mrs. Lothian's. It would have been nice could you and Natalie have gone over Easter Monday.

I think I sent you her address and now I suppose you would like to hear something about how we are being entertained in this bachelor's quarters.

Mr. Branette met us at the 5:30 train yesterday and it took about ½ hour to drive home. It is a pretty house way in from the road. A room each side of front door, one a sitting-room. Back of it is dining room with one end a large bay window. Our room is over it and the bay part makes a pretty porch on which you get a fine view of Ocean and there hangs a hammock. The house was trimmed with smilax and beautiful flowers. The dinner table looked so pretty! Our napkins were tied with different colored ribbons. The finger bowls had orange blossoms in. Our room had even pen, ink and paper and stamped envelopes; thought I'd not use them however. He even had cologne and flowers. I tell you all these things because it isn't often men are so thoughtful. He had for dinner very fine sugar roast beef, potatoes, chicken croquettes, ripe tomatoes with a splendid dressing, tea and wine. Then for desert, strawberries and cream, pie, oranges, and nuts. He made and cooked everything himself. He lives all alone—only a Chinaman to work on the place. It seems so queer. He is a man of means, has lived abroad, and traveled all over. He is about 39 or 40, I guess. He has gray hair and black eyes and moustache. His place was all in apricots last year. They dried eleven tons. The pits are used for fuel. On our way out we passed a lima bean field 9 miles long and 2 wide. Now I must close for Max and I are about to get dinner. Had long letter from Lydia. Did you read that in Dr. Bailey's paper, "Do Children Pray?" it was open there and was real sweet.

Oh how I want to see you.

Lovingly
M

(There is the most beautiful pink passion flower over front of the house. I will bring seeds.)

Chapter 44

Letter Twenty-Six

Mr. Branette, Max, and Fred are going to town right after lunch so I'll just add a line to what I wrote yesterday. Max is fixing lunch. You would like him so much. He is so neat about himself and then when he has time he improves himself by reading & c. I had to laugh at him when we were cleaning up the breakfast! He said, "Do you know Mrs. Smythe, I use to think before I ever had any of this kind of work to do, that women were so slow, but I don't any more." From your account I fear poor Natalie had her hands full to get you cleaned up for I know how dusty and dirty things get, just from Fri. to Fri., with a little everyday brushing up.

Do you think you will be fortunate enough to have another chance to go up home, or to come for me and go back? If so, we could stop over a train or two and see Mrs. Phipps with Freda.

We thought it very odd that Abe's[50] Money Order should have come to your notice. As Fred often says this world is small.

Do you think Fredericka will know her Mama? I judge from you letter she knew you.

Tell Mr. Wine for me this is a trip I know he would enjoy taking with Luke, and that you are going to take someday with your daughter if God lets you both live. It costs frightfully, but our ship will come in some day.

Lunch is ready so with love I must close

Your wife
M

Chapter 45

Letter Twenty-Seven

Ventura
April 11, 1891

My dear Geo

How good you are to write. I received one yesterday and the day before, April 3 and 4. Was more than sorry to hear of Natalie's cold and know the Porter's were disappointed not to have her. I'm also sorry she got such a bad opinion of Ike for he talks that way as much to tease the folks as anything for he is just as good hearted as he can be. He calls Fredericka "our baby." Says she "has nice fat little cheeks" and c & c. Poor fellow; I feel sorry for him and it must make him feel bad when he sees other children especially at the same table his own little ones used to be so happy at. You remember, I've told you he used to take almost entire care of them, to be sure they always had a nurse, but often I've seen him leave a game of cards and go put them to bed instead of allowing the nurse or a

(Sentence ends abruptly here.)

I have been out driving all the morning with Mr. Branette and now must finish this before lunch because just after they will start for town for mail and such, and, although this is not worth sending I know you would rather have it than nothing.

Mr. Branette has two colts which will be broken this fall, but now he uses an old one and with a buggy, we only can go one at a time. I wish I could enclose you some of his own canned apricots. I never tasted better!

Give enclosed to Natalie and love to James and much to yourself.

Yours with haste
M

Chapter 46

Letter Twenty-Eight

Ventura
Sun. April 12

How many more Sundays will it be I wonder before I'll be with my own blessed husband and darling child? No one knows how I long to see them. We have not been to church. Fred has gone to ride with a man that used to live in Kansas. Mr. Branette took Max, who has LaGripp[51] to see the doctor. Tomorrow we go on a picnic up the Canyon; start at 8 A.M. The time passes rapidly, although it is more quiet here than where we've been in the evening. We play cards or "twiddley-winks."

Yesterday Fred received letter from Lydia Remsley in answer to one he wrote expressing his sympathy. It seems to have pleased her, although his was a queer one. In it he said, "You know I have never loved you." But aside from that, it was kindness itself. She feels Josh is not improving. The N.Y. affair is likely to turn out better than she hoped. Jones was willing to send back draft for $2,500 and $2,200 of the other.

I'm so sorry for Annie Lothian. Has not God been merciful to us, darling, for we are free from trouble, but of our friends.

You have twice kindly offered to send me a Money Order. I though possibly I could manage without your sending, for Aunt Emily has let me pay only for the little gifts I've bought for different ones. Wouldn't even let me pay for my wash, but I've broken my glasses twice, have bought two or three small pieces of jewelry, a silver spoon, and many *little things. So, if you can just as well as not, I'd be glad to have a little on reaching Denver or Hays City. I will let you know in time to get it there. I was reading in "Once a Week" quite an interesting article on "Lost Money Orders." Was surprised that the system was only established in 1864. It said the Government had made nearly $2,000,000 above the legitimate profits through failure of orders being presented for payment.*

I have intended writing to Mrs. Summy ever since our visit to St. Joseph, so think I will today. Will write a little home now with fondest love and so much of it. I am your own wife always and forever. Give love to Natalie and James. I hope her cold has left.

M

Chapter 47

Letter Twenty-Nine

Ventura, April 14, 1891
Tuesday A M

Dearest

Aunt Emily and Fred have gone to take a look at the place next to Mr. Branette's that Fred thinks of buying. So I'll write you about our picnic yesterday which we enjoyed very much. We drove about 15 miles, crossed a little river 8 times and how I wished for you on account of the trout fishing you could have indulged in. We could even see the shy little things. On the way out we saw some date-palms over 100 years old for they were planted by the Mission Fathers. There is one of the Mission Churches in town. The old chimes you can hear out here.

I was unfortunate enough to again break my glasses yesterday making the 3ʳᵈ time. With a Money Order I would not have to be identified as with a registered letter would, and if I wouldn't I would be glad to have it at Salt Lake City.

You ask if we are going to the Yosemite. Oh, yes for as one gentleman said to us, "...to come to California and not go there was like Shakespeare without Hamlet." The Valley is now open and we will go there on way to Salt Lake.

I wrote to you yesterday so you will excuse this for not containing much. I received your's yesterday with Mrs. Lothian's. Was quite surprised. Yes, I know the Porter's were disappointed not to have

Natalie. You and James must take very good care of her for colds go hard with her. I had a very bad one for nearly three weeks taken on my way out. It was so provoking for it was the only one I have had this winter. Also received one from Mrs. Prather.

I am growing just as anxious to see you as you are to see me. Fred says to tell you that we will have to walk home if we are not there by June 7th for our ticket is not good after that date. So after we leave here I shall feel as if it would not take us long to reach home. We have been here 1 week and the rest has been good for Aunt Emily.

Fondly your's.

Much love to Natalie.

Expect to leave here day after tomorrow.

Mamie

Chapter 48

Mary politely refused Fred's invitation for an evening stroll on Ventura's pristine and desolate beach, and it infuriated him. "What has become of you, Mary?" Fred demanded an answer. "You've withdrawn from me, and I don't like it one bit. I'm trying to be patient, Mary, and I will be, but darling, you've become so distant. Please talk to me."

She consented that she owed him that much. She knew she needed to speak the truth into *those eyes* and let him know that she had reached a decision.

"I'm not staying in California, Fred. I have a husband and daughter who need me, and whom I love dearly. I need to return to Maryland as soon as possible." Mary spoke softly then added, "Let's walk out through the gardens."

He held the door open for her and she gathered her skirts and slipped past him into the cool evening air. She affixed her shawl around her shoulders and continued, "You knew all along I could not stay. You can't be too terribly surprised." She tried to sound matter-of-fact, yet sympathetic.

"I hoped beyond hope you would not return." Fred kept his head bowed as it had been, and never took his eyes off the path. "I though I could persuade you to stay." He stopped and looked at her. "I thought you *wanted* to stay." His voice trailed off as he returned his gaze to the moss-encrusted brick walkway and slowly walked on.

Mary slipped her hand through his arm, as she had done for many, many years. "I did consider it." She paused. "But, I can't go against my conscience. It would be wrong; wrong in so many ways."

They slowly strolled, arm in arm, without saying a word.

Fred broke the silence. "Can you honestly tell me you *don't* love me? Was I so utterly mistaken during the past few weeks? Have I been completely amiss all through the years?"

She didn't know how to answer, however she knew she'd better choose her words very carefully. She took her time and walked in the direction of a park bench facing the water. She sat, and he sat next to her.

"I have always loved you, Fred. You know that. And," she hesitated before adding, "I suppose I always will." She kept her gaze fixed on the sea. "But that doesn't mean we can ever be together." She reiterated, "Ever."

"What's changed?"

"Things like *integrity* and *faithfulness* are enduring qualities. Fulfillment of misdirected love would bring temporary pleasure, but would be ultimately destructive to so many people." She paused. "Fred, you do see that, don't you?"

"Is that what you see our love to be, 'misdirected'?"

"Yes." Her reply was simple and to the point, but nonetheless painful.

"I see," he said as he stood and took a few steps away from the bench. "'Misdirected'."

"I'm *married*," she stressed and said in a raised voice. "And I *love* my husband, and my daughter. I won't do anything that will hurt them any more than I already have. I've done enough damage already. Besides, I don't think the Lord wants us to exchange our long-term commitments for temporary pleasures."

"Oh, yes, *the Lord*. I didn't realize I was up against *Him*, too." Fred tensed his dark eyebrows and furrowed his forehead as if deep in thought. A few minutes later he added, "Don't you think *the Lord* wants us to be happy? Don't you think *the Lord* wants us to satisfy our longing for each other and be together? After all, *He* made us and gave us our desire for one another."

She wasn't long in answering. "Actually, no I don't." Mary replied in a very confident, calm, and upbeat voice. She stood up and squarely faced those eyes, that just a short time ago had been so terribly unsettling. "I may have tried to convince myself that at one time," she said shaking her head 'no', "but I don't feel that way any longer. I've come to realize that it's not our temporary pleasure that He's as concerned with as it is our obedience and steadfast faithfulness to Him."

With a somewhat sheepish look, Fred bit his lower lip and nodded in agreement. He took a deep breath in and sighed out slowly.

"I admire your tenacity, Mary. You're a strong woman. I think one day you'll regret not staying here with me, but I will respect your wishes…and I will *always* love you."

Chapter 49

Letter Thirty

Ventura
Noon April 15ᵗʰ

Dearest

Your's containing check came yesterday after I'd sent yours. Mr. Branette will have it cashed at the Ventura Bank when he and Fred go there this afternoon. It was so kind and good of you to send without my asking and I appreciate it more than had it been a hundred and I had to ask for it, for I'd rather do without unless it is for the baby or house than to ask.

I wonder, darling, why you were feeling as you did that day. You remember you said you had made several attempts to write, but each would have made me feel bad. I can't imagine why it was unless I had said something in my letter. If so, please forgive, for it was unintentional my own dear George. I fear it must have been that for with Natalie in the nest, Abigail to keep her from being lonely, I know it wasn't house affairs to worry about and Fredericka is well. Oh, how I wish I could put my arms about your neck and look into your dear face and I then could read it all I'm sure.

But now let me give you our plans and if it was your two little girls you were homesick to have back in the nest, you will see how soon it will be, God willing. We leave tomorrow—5:25 P.M. for Santa Barbara where we remain a few days. Then, on the 27ᵗʰ we start for

Yosemite Valley. Fred has such a fearful cold, he is afraid to go into the Valley before that. About the 4th or 5th of May we will reach Salt Lake so I see I've had you write there a little early, however it will be lovely to know some letters will be awaiting us.

I won't take time to tell you the other dates today; will in my next, however we now think to reach home May 20th. Now, that is better than June 15th.

If Natalie is going, keep her till she is entirely well. I fear her colds. Give her my best love.

Your own
M

Chapter 50

Letter Thirty-One

The Arlington Hotel[52]
Santa Barbara, Cal.
11:30 a.m. April 17, 1891

My dearest Geo

How I wish I had you here by me that you might see these beautiful mountains dotted with pretty cottages!

We left Mr. Branette's at 4:00 p.m. yesterday with the same team that took us on our picnic. Mr. Miller, the owner, told us he had been fishing up there the afternoon before and caught 35 trout. The train ran right by the Sea on our left and on the right was the mountains and cultivated fields. In that 3-mile bean field I told you of, we saw them cultivating using 48 horses.

We reached here 6:30. Have a splendid room with parlor. Fred and Max are near. Have marked ours[53]. This morn was the first they were ready for breakfast before us, so when we went to dining room, Fred had on his Mother's place a beautiful bunch of mixed roses and at mine pink. After it, he and I went to where they have California woods for sale. The owner explained them to us and what they went through & c. It was very interesting. Fred bought a ruler. It cost $4. Just to think there are 100 or more woods in this state. He is to furnish a room for Mrs. Stanford.

Have just time to mail this. Going out to ride after lunch.

Yours with fondest love

Chapter 51

"You both have had such dreadful colds." Aunt Emily's observations started the morning's conversation at the breakfast table. "Honestly, I thought this was supposed to be such a *healthy* place." Her comments seemed especially comical as she added heaps of fresh-churned butter to the already decadently rich breakfast pastry. "Where did I read that? Harper's? Or was it Ladies Home Journal? I know I read it somewhere. Regardless, you couldn't prove it by the two of you. Dreadful colds. Just think how sick you'd be if we hadn't had all this fresh fruit every day. And sunshine. Goodness! Later on why don't the two of you take a nice long walk on the beach? The fresh air will do you both good. Splendid idea." She repeated herself with much more enthusiasm. "Splendid idea!"

Fred and Mary's eyes met across the table and they both smirked. Fred winked at Mary, and she broke into a grin. They both knew that whenever Aunt Emily thought she'd come up with a 'splendid idea', there was no rest for anyone until that plan was fulfilled.

"You've been telling us to take 'nice long walks…in the fresh air' all our lives, Mother." Fred replied dryly as he added maple syrup to his oatmeal, but this time he, too, thought it a 'splendid idea'. "I agree. We won't have many more days like this; I think it's a wonderful idea. What do you think Mary? Up for a nice walk?"

She raised an eyebrow and glanced up at him with a little half-smile. "I think that would be lovely." Her reply was quite unemotional, and for the first time in many days, she actually felt unemotional. "I'd like to take my journal and see if I can add some more specimens to my wildflower collection."

"I'm very relieved that you aren't furious with me." Mary's words were soft-spoken and sincere as they walked along the edge of the shore. "I know you think I'm making the wrong decision, but it would be all the more difficult if you turned against me. I would hate that."

"I'd never turn against you, Mary. I am very disappointed, of course…but not furious." He paused. "Like I told you, I will *always* love you, Mary. Nothing will ever change that. I know you really think you are in love with George and are convinced that is where you want to be, or where you think you should to be. As much as I hate to admit it, you probably are doing what is best for Fredericka, but I'm not at all convinced it will bring you happiness."

Mary was stunned by this admission, and somewhat relieved. At least he'd found some value in her decision.

"Please just don't avoid me, dear. *Please* don't cut me out of your and Freddie's lives." Fred's request was a plea from the bottom of his heart. He took her hand and stepped directly in front of her so she could step no further. "I *promise* you I won't overstep my bounds, Mary, just don't push me away. I couldn't bear that. Please. Promise me; just promise me that much."

Those eyes. Blast it! Mary closed her own piercingly dark eyes so as not to have to look into his quite yet. She could feel the warm tears welling up and a lump in her throat. Blast it! She didn't want to cry now. Not now! She needed to be strong, but her tears had already spilled over. "I promise." Her voice cracked, and he instantly retrieved from his pocket a crisp handkerchief with a monogrammed "D" and wiped away her tears.

She turned her head and laid it, and her open hands, on his broad chest. "I won't ever push you away." She spoke so softly to his beating heart, she didn't know if he even heard her.

He wrapped his arms around her, held her close, and gently patted her on the back. With her eyes closed, she sobbed quietly and gently on his chest.

Without a further word spoken, somehow, deep within, they both knew this was the last time they would ever hold each other this way again.

Chapter 52

Letter Thirty-Two

The Arlington Hotel
Santa Barbara, Cal.
April 18, 1891

My dear Husband,

Oh, how I want to see you this Saturday eve, but you are thousands of miles from me! All I'd say must be in writing. First, I'd tell you how much I love you (I'd try to). Then I'd tell you of all we've seen today, for right after breakfast we went to drive.

First visited the old Mission which is said to be the best preserved one of the 24 which was founded by the Franciscan Fathers. We saw several of the monks walking about with their brown gowns and hoods. Then we drove through the city and into the beautiful Montecito Valley. There were lovely homes all through. We drove through several of the private grounds. One was a nephew's of Jay Gould's[54]. He had 300 kinds of trees; of course, not all natives of this state. Then we drove into a widow's place where we saw a grape vine 50 years old. Said to be the largest in the world grown out of doors. There are three very large ones in Europe at the Courts, but under glass. This one has about 8,000 lbs. of grapes a season. One bunch weighing 15 lbs., so we were told. I rather doubt it! Around some of the places their hedges would be made of roses; others it would be of geraniums growing 6 or 7 feet high. From all these grand homes you could catch glimpses of the Sea.

A gentleman who lives in Baltimore was seated at our table at dinner tonight. He looks like Ike D. somewhat.

April 19, 1891

This morning Aunt Emily and I went to Grace Methodist Church. Heard two excellent addresses from young men. The Y.M.C.A. of Lower California are holding their convention here. I imagine they originally came from the east. One had attended Princeton. It is a large church. I never saw so many Methodist ones as they have in this state!

Aunt Emily has gone to a women's meeting there this afternoon, but Fred wanted to take me to the beach. He and Max went this a.m., so I went with him, although I would much rather have gone to church or remained in and written to you. However, we can't always please ourselves and he went only because he thought it would give me pleasure. And it gave me a chance to speak to him about his smoking, for he won't let his Mother say a word! And, oh, it is just awful the way he keeps it up! I truly think it will kill him. I told him about the Lawrence brothers that died. I'd be ashamed to be born a man and be a slave to any habit. It is bad enough to be a woman and be so weak minded, but a man is supposed to be stronger in every way. We gathered sea mosses for the book I'm making of California wild-flowers and mosses[55]. He gathered me some beauties this morning!

On the way back, we went through Chinatown and went into their Josh House.[56] Tomorrow at 11 a.m. we take a 14 mile drive to the Hot Springs. Max on horseback.

How I want to see my big boy and little girl[57]! Do you know I hope we'll all go to Heaven together? It would be so hard to be left or to go and leave my treasures.

Have enclosed list as near as we can now tell where we expect to be on named dates.

Forever yours

Photo of original flowers Mary and Fred gathered and pressed.

Chapter 53

Letter Thirty-Three

Arlington Hotel
Santa Barbara, Cal.
April 21, 1891

My dear Geo

We leave at 4:10 for Ventura, and while waiting will commence a letter even if I've not time to finish. I want to tell you about our trip yesterday to the Hot Springs where we had dinner at the Hotel and tasted the hot sulfur waters but did not bathe. It is 1500 ft. The view is grand! You see the valley and sea, but the mist only lifted for about 80 seconds. It was a disappointment to us.

On our return the driver left Aunt Emily and I at the Faith Mission to see a Mrs. Schludder, the lady in charge of this, another one of Dr. Cullen's grand works. It is for a home for young men where they can have board for $4.50 a week or for nothing if they are without means. Has a free reading-room. A pretty chapel. President Harrison will arrive here Friday. They are now to work on an arch out in front.

The young man from Baltimore I told you was at our table is a Mr. S. Gordon Olmstead. He is a member of the Baltimore Club.

I just wish I might enclose some of the roses and pinks Fred bought this morning. Also would love to have you taste some of the Japanese plum or Loquat; an entire new fruit to me. Although they have them in New Orleans and you may have had them. Nearly every hour in the day

142

*there is something I wish you might taste or see. Down by the porch
there is a rose tree. It is 27 inches in circumference.*

*We went to the woodworkers again and on way over Fred killed a
gofer.*

*Aunt Emily bought you an article as near as what you told her to
bring as she*

(Mary's letter ends unfinished here.)

Chapter 54

Letter Thirty-Four

Rose Hotel, Ventura
Wednesday noon
April 22nd, 1891

The carriage was ready to take us to train before I had finished and as I was so sure of finding a letter here from you I didn't mail it, but, I was doomed to disappointment for on arriving Fred received note from Mr. Branette saying he had taken our mail out to the Ranch. We think he thought we would come right on out or early this morning although Fred had said when we left him last Thursday that we would remain here over night. Aunt Emily and I are in hopes to go out only to take lunch and then Mr. Branette would give Fred the room he gave us for Fred added very much to his cold out there. You see, they don't build out here for cold and this season is three weeks backward they tell us. I think it wonderful that a bachelor could take care of four as well as he did and we all think he entertained us long enough, but he seems very anxious to have us return and I don't know how it will be settled. Fred and Max drove out in a buggy right after breakfast. Mr. Thorne is there from Los Angeles waiting to see Fred for he has decided to buy the place of his. So we will be obliged to remain till Monday a.m. to have papers and everything fixed.

This hotel is owned by the Mr. Rose that was on our train when we crossed the Continent; the one who raises race horses and owns the Ranch next to Lucky Baldwin's. You would be amazed to see how handsomely it is furnished; more than any Hotel we have stopped at; like a private house. There are three or four other hotels in town.

I will mail this when I go down to lunch and not wait till the boys come back with our mail. We told Mr. Branette not to remail to us at Santa Barbara so you see I've not heard from you since the 8th when you seemed to feel blue. I'll write again when I get yours.

Fondly your wife
M

Oh I want to see you so much!
I'll write again to Natalie when I know her address.
Did you take any interest in the Whist[58] *Congress held at Milwaukee?*

Chapter 55

Letter Thirty-Five

Ventura
Thursday, April 23rd 1891

The boys brought back our mail yesterday 4 PM but I'd mailed yours and I was very happy at having two from you. I think by this time you are receiving mine regularly for I write about every other day. Also had one from Laura. Said Natalie wrote Madelyn she was very lonesome. So I imagine by this time you are alone. I do trust you engaged Lulie before Natalie left. It would be so much more like home for you and James for, from your letters I judge he never went to board with Mrs. Barr.

I smiled when you mentioned "My tale of woe." I knew that before. Had not told you as I didn't think "the man that knows it all" need be told such things. Laura wrote me that Mrs. Felicia Hammond had lost her hopes. Now I guess you don't know that, or Mrs. Hammond would have told that to Natalie. I suppose I ought to answer Mrs. Lothian's letter.

Mr. Branette is determined we shall return to his place. The boys say he is all trimmed again with flowers in every room. At 11 A.M. we drive out there, but return here on Saturday so to start early Monday.

They write William Deats' wife is dead. The baby is very well. Ike is very fond of her; loves to kiss her and have her call him. Laura says she is just lovely.

I forgot to tell you that San Buenaventura in Spanish means Good Venture.

In the Ladies Home Journal for March I saw enclosed advertisement for wall papers. How would it do to send for them? It is time to put on my hat, so fondly

Yours always,
M

Chapter 56

Letter Thirty-Six

Rose Hotel, Ventura
Saturday 4 PM
April 25, 1891

My ever dear Geo

We have just got in from Mr. Branette's. Our second visit has been as delightful as the first. I am so anxious that you two should meet. Fred says he thinks him to be one of the truest gentlemen he ever met. He ought to know for he was with him so much abroad. Well, I think it true, for he never seems to forget himself. The day we drove out (Thursday), after a delicious lunch which he had prepared, he took us through the place where the fruit is attended to.

Yesterday I spent in sewing, for traveling so much is frightfully hard on one's dresses.

Mr. Branette and Fred drove in to see the President.[59] People from near and far were at the train. About 750 school children were there to pelt the car with flowers. I must tell you about our riding over flowers today! Just as we were leaving, Aunt Emily said she wanted to see the spot Fred had marked for his house, so returning past Mr. Branette's, he had thrown the greatest lot of callas, roses, & c. for us to drive over!

I suppose you have commenced writing to Salt Lake. It does seem so long to wait to hear.

We had a good laugh at your remark about sending out cards, and being married again! Fred says we must select another "best man" for he can't be there.[60] *Well, in a way it will seem a little like commencing again, but we have gained two things since then: Our darling baby. And experience. And now that we are making a new start, shall we try and let our experience teach us to be more patient with each other, for the sake of that little one who has been given us to raise, and then for James' sake. For I know several times since he has been with us we must have made it very unpleasant for him. Of course, way down in our hearts we loved each other as much as ever, only those mean things we said, and so often have I wished them back.*[61] *Last evening I was reading one of Carlton's poems and I'm going to try and remember this verse.*

"Boys flying kites haul in their white-winged birds
You can't do that way when you're flying words
'Careful with fire' is good advice, we know;
'Careful with words' is ten times doubly so
Thoughts unexpressed may sometimes fall back dead
But God Himself can't kill them when they're said."

And now, darling, if God brings me back to your dear arms in safety, by His help, I'll try and be a better little wife. If not, He will forgive the past.

Sunday 5 PM April 26, 1891

This A.M. Aunt Emily and I went to St. Paul's Episcopal Church; found service not till night. Fred went too. So then went to Presbyterian. Heard good sermon. John 14 chapter 22 verse. Said it was impossible for us all to see alike. Even the Bible didn't read the same to one man as to another.

After lunch Fred, Aunt Emily, and I walked through a lovely garden and now Mr. Branette has arrived to dine with us. He and Fred have gone to walk.

Last evening a Mrs. Briggs (husband owns a ranch near Fred's) gave me some flowers that were to have been given Mrs. President Harrison!

I wonder dearest, where you are today. When are you going down to see Dr. Summy?

After we leave here, we shall have taken our last look at the Pacific. Give love to Mrs. Hammond and Natalie if in Hyattsville.

Chapter 57

Mary stepped out of her little slipper and propped her tiny toes on the dry rock just above the high-tide line. She raised her skirts and rolled down her stocking, and then repeated the same on her other leg. She turned and sat against the rock and removed her hose from her feet and put them neatly, one in each shoe. She wiggled her toes in the sand and smiled as she looked out to sea. It has been a good trip overall, she thought to herself, and smiled. Yes, a very good trip, but she was missing George and her longing for her daughter was indescribable. It was time to go home.

She stood and bent over at the waist, and reached between her ankles to grab the hem of the back of her skirts. As she stood up, she pulled the back hem up between her legs and tucked it in her front waistband, effectively leaving her unencumbered from her knees down. She took her time walking the short distance to the water's edge, and stood ankle deep in the lapping water. Once again, for an undetermined time, she just stared out over the water, this time thanking the Lord for the beauty of His earth, for their safety thus far, and for her little family waiting for her back home. She felt freer than she ever remembered feeling and certainly closer to the Lord. She knew her time away had changed her and she was returning home with a newfound love for her husband and a recommitment to her Lord.

"I thought I would find you here." That smooth, deep voice that had so recently melted her heart interrupted her quiet time and startled her a little. She didn't know that her cousin had been watching her from the lawn the entire time.

"I had to get my feet wet one more time." Mary was surprised when she heard the crack in her own voice. "The sea is so beautiful." She paused and then added, "I want George and Freddie to see all this some day."

Fred picked up a little rock or a shell or something and heaved it out into the water. Then another one and another behind that. "Are you sure you're ready to go back?"

"I'm positive." She smiled a broad smile and looked right up at those eyes. She nodded her head and added, "I'm sure."

Simultaneously they began slowly walking down the water's edge, stopping only to sort through the little undiscovered treasures that had washed up. Fred occasionally hurled something back into the sea as if trying to throw off some unexplained weight, but Mary kept silent. Perhaps this unfamiliar response would serve her well in the future. Keeping quiet certainly did not come naturally to her.

"Your new ranch is beautiful, Fred, and the spot you've chosen to build your home is simply amazing. The view is spectacular." She tried as hard as she could to sound excited but realized her tone did not quite measure up. "Why, you're going to grow the finest oranges anywhere!" There, that sounded more encouraging, she thought. "Do you think you'll add apricots?"

He looked at her as if she had just asked the single dumbest question on earth. Obviously, he wasn't thinking about apricots, she concluded.

"I don't know about that. It's too soon to tell." Fred's reply was perfectly flat. "Branette said he can set me up with other growers in the area who can advise me on the specifics."

"Thank you for all the flowers." Mary changed the subject. "Oh! And, all those flowers in the drive yesterday were such a treat! How'd you ever come up with that?"

"If it was good enough for President and Mrs. Harrison, then it was befitting of you, my dear."

They smiled, glanced at each other, and walked on for some time.

"Are you alright here alone, Mary?" Fred's concern and question was very sincere and genuine.

"I'm fine. Really I am." She nodded, assuring him as she stopped, smiled just a little, and looked up at him. "I'm fine. I really just need to be alone for a little while, OK?" she added.

She didn't realize that she furrowed her eyebrows and pinched her lips tightly together, but Fred recognized that she was very near tears.

"That's fine, honey. Take all the time you want; we're in no rush at all." Fred's voice was so soft and compassionate, and he truly did know her and understand her better than anyone; he loved her. He turned and started to walk back. He took a few steps toward the grand lawn, then turned back to her and simply said, "Mary."

She turned her head toward him, and then he added with conviction in his voice, "Just be sure."

Chapter 58

Letter Thirty-Seven

10:20 a.m. Ventura April 27th

This will be my last for a few days. I have such a strange feeling about entering the Valley, but it would be mean for me to tell you just how I feel, for you might worry. I suppose it is because I am more homesick than I have been any time before. I do enjoy your bag so much that you gave me before we were married.

We are waiting for the bus to take us to train, and they are all talking about me, and I can't write so darling goodbye. God bless and keep you and bring us soon together.

Your wife in life or death
M

Chapter 59

Letter Thirty-Eight

The Wawona Hotel[62]
Mariposa Co., Cal.
Tues 8 p.m., April 28, 1891

Dearest

I am sorry I sent you rather a blue letter yesterday but I couldn't help it for I had such a queer feeling about coming here, or rather, the Valley. We had to leave our sleeper at this a.m. at 3:40. The Porter was to call us in time but he didn't, consequently we arrived at Berenda before my dress was on or hair combed. I got the skirt on, a shawl around me and my hat on. I was a sight but our party, two other gentlemen and the moon were the only ones to behold your crazy looking wife. Had to wait 2 hours for Raymond train where a good, hot breakfast awaited us and at 7:30 the 2 stages drove up. Our party and the other people (one as large as Sam[63]) occupied one; another party the other. Each stage had 4 horses. These were changed 4 times before dinner at Sulphour Springs. That was 15 miles, then there to here 12 more, so we are very tired and I will finish this in the morning dear.

Chapter 60

Letter Thirty-Nine

The Wawona Hotel
Mariposa Co., Cal.
Wed. April 29th 11 A.M. 1891

Fred, Max, & I have been out for a walk. We all spoke of how you would enjoy the trout fishing. We could see them darting about; had some for breakfast. The rest of the party left at 7 o'clock for the Valley but we thought on Aunt Emily's account it best to wait over till tomorrow for rest. After we have lunch at 12, we leave to see the big trees 8 miles off. Then back here for the night and make our start tomorrow. This is a splendidly kept house. From my window I can see the snow on the mountain nearby. We seemed odd yesterday to drive through snow. (over I mean) Just a little. I don't wonder now that it is so expensive a trip for the building such a stage route was fearful. At Berenda where we leave the main line, the tickets were $45 a piece. Every meal is $1 a piece and I don't know the hotel charges.

When I told you I'd not write from the Valley I didn't think I'd be able to, but as I can, I knew you would be glad to know I was feeling bright again. Will write tonight and tell you about the trees.

7 P. M.

I told you I'd tell you about the Big trees after the visit, but darling, I can't. Have no words to make you realize them. They are simply I M M E N S E. I measured with a string around the base of one called the Grizzly Giant. Will show you on our lawn how big it measured and if the lawn isn't large enough, why, we'll borrow the White lot. By the way, our pretty lawn must begin to look lovely by this time. And how would it do to have some way of not running over that path that is already quite noticeable, for do you know, since seeing so many flowers, a green lawn is more than ever my idea of a neat place.

We start at 7 a.m. tomorrow and I must get to bed early. Have breakfast at six. I am to write home now, so, dearest, good night.

Only three weeks more and I'll be with you or at least very near you. God willing.

My love to James.

Faithfully your loving wife

Chapter 61

Letter Forty

Yosemite April 30th

My dear Geo,

Don't you think I'm doing very well in the writing line after telling you I was not going to write while in the Valley? But it is all so different from what I expected! The hotels have every convenience for so doing, and then I am enjoying it so immensely and you know I thought I wouldn't, so I feel each day like trying to tell you a little of what I see, and, as I asked you to keep my letters, it will be the same as if I was writing in my diary.

Well, this morn we left at seven. Two other gentlemen in our stage. One was Shepard Knapp, Jr. of New York. You know the carpet firm. He kindly had me take his box-seat (by the driver) when we were about to enter the valley. You speak ahead for choice of seats, and the driver was just splendid to tell me everything. Such a sight—I'll never forget it!

As soon as we arrived, Fred spoke for saddle horses and after lunch the party except Aunt Emily started for Vernal and Nevada Falls[64]. Can't drive. There were six men counting guide and I the only lady, so I had all the attention. We went up 1900 feet. Some places like steps but the horses and mules know so well where to place their feet. Coming down I felt many times I should pitch over its head. It fully paid and I'll show you all about it.

158

We get off at 6 a.m. in the morning for Wawona where we stay all night and leave for Raymond 8 a.m. Sat. That eve we get on our sleeper and arrive at Sacramento early Sun. Will spend the day there, but have to leave at 11 p.m. so to reach Salt Lake Tuesday. Will write on Sun.

I get so tired seeing so much. I can't half tell you all I'd like to when night comes, but I can when I see you dearest.

Your loving M

Chapter 62

Letter Forty-One

Dearest

We have just arrived; were an hour late in leaving Berenda, our sleeper was on side track till 5 this morn. Have a large corner room and will rest here till 11 PM. Aunt Emily and I thought to go to church here this a.m. but she is too tired and is now sleeping. I'm so thankful to think she has stood the Valley trip and that we are out of it although it was delightful. So much staging was hard. Friday morn on leaving the Valley we suddenly heard a low rumbling sound which grew louder and resembled a train in a tunnel. The driver (Stevens) drew in his horses. I watched his face closely for I was startled. He assured us it was a long ways off and was either a land or snow slide. Every spring men are sent over the sides to inspect, so to make the trails safe. A Mrs. Stewart of New York who was in the 2nd stage the day we started was brought out sick. They've been in their own car.

8 P.M.

Aunt Emily is taking another nap. Fred and Max have gone for a walk and now I'm going to tell you about the Chinese woman's funeral Fred and I attended at 2:30. In front of her house there was a booth covered with white muslin. On a large table was a roast pig, another that was not, a lamb, a fish, any number of sweet stuffs, bowls of boiled rice, burning candles and tapers & c. Most of this was taken to the grave. On an express wagon were piled her things. These also went there where they were burned after the priest (or whatever he was) had finished his racket on the clappers and the coffin was lowered in grave (without a box). They took the eatables and some of the dishes and threw in the fire and I have one of the bowls. Isn't it well to be born lucky? Fred says he believes I've never wished for a thing but I'd get it. Said if he had gone out alone, he would never have run into that. Haven't half told you all but it will keep.

This photo of Mary was taken while on this trip
and is believed to have been taken at Yosemite.

Chapter 63

Letter Forty-Two

May 4, 1891
On Sleeper

You said you could not read what I wrote on car before so I'll write again for at Salt Lake there may not be much time for writing, but, oh, how glad I shall be to get letters from you and to hear of Fredericka. I think I may have told you rather too soon to write to Salt Lake, but I shall be the better off tomorrow. I might have had you direct longer to Ventura, but we didn't just know when we would leave so yours of April 12th was the last I've had. Imagine how I long for tomorrow. There are several little tots on the different sleepers. I see them as we pass through to dining car and how it makes me wish for my baby. It is well we are on the homeward way or it would make me miserable enough. There is little to interest you along here. We are now passing along by the course of the Truckee River and can see the Humboldt Mountains[65]. There are a great many people going east now. I have an idea Fred would like to have remained longer. He would have liked to have seen the Geysers north of San Francisco. You remember you thought I was mistaken about them.

With a heart full of love, I am your own faithful
M

Chapter 64

Letter Forty-Three

The Cullen
Salt Lake City
May 5, 1891

Dearly Beloved

Maybe I ought to be in bed rather than writing, but the door is closed into Aunt Emily's room so I know my light won't trouble her, and I can't sleep until I tell you how more than happy your 6 precious letters received today have made me, especially the one of the 25th. I was filled with "A feeling that declines to be described." Yes, darling, I have prayed often about it[66], and I am coming home now with the lightest, gayest, and most thankful heart you can imagine!

Shall I now give you an account of today? Well, we reached Ogden at 6.30 where we had breakfast. Then took train for here. It took about an hour. On the way we passed the Mineral Springs. We came to this hotel because Mrs. Anderson (Mrs. McCoy's daughter) was here. Found she had left on Sunday and the Judge was away holding Court. Mrs. Anderson's brother died 30 days after coming out.

We sent Max right to P.O. I could scarcely wait for his return and had I known of my surprise in store, I would have been even more impatient, but with the sweet we must have some bitter and mine came in.

Poor Lydia. I enclose it. I don't know what to write her next. Fred told his Mother she ought to write and tell her their home was open to her at any time. If Josh is released, of course things will be in an awful state. I really fear, brave as she has been, she will soon break under it.

Had good news from all other letters and from my own dear baby. After reading our letters, we had lunch then took a drive all around first stopping at the Tabernacle. It seats 12,000. It is 233 feet long and we at one end could hear a pin drop at the other. The temple you know is not yet finished, has up to date cost $3,500,000. Then we drove to The Tithing Building, which is a general depot for taxes collected by the Mormon Church from its disciples. Then we saw what was once Brigham's domains, the Beehive, and Lion House, his grave, Amelia Palace that he built for his favorite wife & c. From Prospect Hill we had a fine view of the City and its surroundings. We were fortunate in having a very talkative old driver. Even did a little singing. He must have told us all there was to tell and I'll try and remember it all to tell you darling, when we get back. I stopped with Aunt Emily while she had her feet fixed.

Chapter 65

Letter Forty-Four

The Cullen
Salt Lake City
May 6, 1891

Aunt Emily, Fred, and I went out to Fort Douglas[67] this a.m. It is three miles out and is the first post Mark was stationed at. Col. Gordon was also there at that time. It is a very pretty post indeed. Tomorrow morn we leave. Before going I will get Max to go before we start to PO and leave word where to forward. Now I'm in a hurry for Denver to hear again from the best, dearest husband I ever had or will have. Two weeks from today we will arrive in Newark early in the A.M. I do hope you can come on; if not, I'll leave for my dear little nest as soon as possible. I can't leave Aunt Emily at Philadelphia. Our things are all mixed and I know she would rather I wouldn't.

Now come near and let me tell you in our own way how happy you have made me and how much you are loved by your own true Mamie.

Love to Natalie. It is awfully kind of her to stay and I know you try to make her happy.

Chapter 66

Letter Forty-Five

Hotel Brunswick
Grand Junction, Colo.
May 8th Friday, 1891

My dear Geo

We reached here 9.30 last eve. Stopped over to rest and be able to pass through Tennessee Pass[68] where we see the Mount of the Holy Cross[69]. We pass through Leadville first. We leave here at 10:10.

Yesterday was the most interesting day we have spent on the train. How I wish you could have seen what is called "Castle Gate."[70] It is two very high pillars of rock. One measures 500 feet and one 400'. After passing through we came out on ledges that looked like castles, forts, and such.

I was only able to write this much yesterday when they said the carriage was ready to take us to the train. It was nearly two hours late. When we reached the Station, a gentleman advised Fred to take the narrow gauge so to see The Black Canyon[71] and Marshall Pass. We would also reach Salida a little earlier. Fred went on from here last night to Denver for he has seen the Royal Pass (Royal Gorge I mean) before and we three remained here all night so to go through there in day-light. Our train being late we could not see any thing of the "Pass" but found it very cold on top, where we waited about 10 minutes in a snow shed. It was made of iron. We were then ten thousand and some feet high.

Before we reached the Black Canon, they put on Observation Cars and oh what a grand ride it was! I'll never be able to tell you half how fine it was. You and Ma I hope and pray may see it all someday. I'll not mail this till reaching Denver where I shall again hear from my dear blessed husband and baby to whom I am now nearing each day and how happy I'm at the thought.

Was so sorry to hear of the death of Mr. Prince. My heart really aches for his wife. They appeared to be such a happy couple. Do you remember how often they used to pass with their children when out walking? Did he leave any thing for his little ones?

Yes, dear, as you say, I truly believe we are as happy as most married people when we are our true selves. Although I know people doubt it when they hear us talk to each other, but God being my helper, I mean to be so careful of my words, if I'm only brought back once more.

I'm so glad we are going to have more blackberries.

You would laugh at the way people mix us up. Some take me for Fred's wife, and then others think I'm his sister and Max is my husband. Then again, we've all been taken for Aunt Emily's grandchildren. It is quite funny!

Chapter 67

Letter Forty-Six

The Albany
Denver, Col.
Sunday, May 10, 1891

Here we are back to this place in safety. Fred, as I wrote you, came on ahead so had a nice room engaged, beautiful flowers in it and our trunk. He had invited Morgan Edgar to dine with him. A young lawyer, his Grandfather was one of Newark's rich men. I was surprised, and disappointed, not to find a line from you, but "No news is good news" and when we reach Hays, I'm sure there will be something from my dear husband. I had excellent news from my baby girl. Fred went to the P.O. this morning to see if there wasn't something there now for me.

Before reaching here I saw there was a telegram awaiting "Mrs. Geo Smythe" and so when reaching the Albany and not finding a word from you, I was naturally alarmed till the telegram was read and found to belong to another Mrs. George Smythe.

Aunt Emily and I went to Trinity Methodist Episcopal Church. Very elegant indeed. The organ is unsurpassed in the new world. When Mrs. Harrison[72] was here, they had her hear it, but what we enjoyed more than that, or the fine building, was the sermon from the pastor. A man about your age. After church, we spoke to him. He was pleasant and had such a kind manner.

Only one more Sunday and I trust we shall be together never again to be separated for so long a time. It seems to me much longer than it

170

has really been for it has been just a little over two months and a half, but that is long enough for me to realize how little life would be without you.

Aunt Emily had a letter from Lydia yesterday and I'm glad to tell you the tone is brighter, although matters are worse, for he has again turned against her. The girl finally saw him. He now insists upon being examined, tried to escape, which has made it worse for him in as much as now the Doctors will not allow him his liberty. It is wonderful how she (Lydia) keeps up. She is a brave, smart woman and we are all proud of her.

I'm anxious to hear if you can meet me. We will reach Newark on Wednesday, May 20th. If you can't come for us, I'll get home to Hyattsville Saturday evening. Aunt Emily says I ought not to hurry off before that. I'll have my trunk to repack. Mr. Branette's family to call on (I promised him to, before leaving Newark) and that will give me time to rest from the trip there from Rock Island and if you come for me I would like to see Eddie.[73] I don't know just when she is to be confined. I doubt if she would like to come in the city to see me. Besides, Aunt Elizabeth[74] has never seen our baby.

I commence to feel quite near you dearest, although I'm many miles off yet. Pray that the Father may bring us the rest of the way also. We pray for you each day. Give love to Natalie and James and take much yourself.

Chapter 68

After returning from the dining car, Fred and Mary sat off by themselves on a deep shade of rose velvet settee at the far end of one of the lavish parlor cars. There were many passengers now traveling east out of Denver, and they came and went unnoticed through the car. Aunt Emily was nowhere to be seen, and again the two were in their own private world. Fred was sipping the finest brandy available and Mary joined him with a little sherry served in delicate etched crystal. This would be a difficult evening for both of them, and they both knew it would be. There was no getting around the fact that Fred's dream was unfulfilled, passion unrequited, and soon he would be separated once again from the love of his life. He would arrive back in Hays tonight and Mary would continue on east to the life she had clearly chosen.

Mary, on the other hand, was quite anxious to be home and to begin to implement all her new intentions as a wife and mother. She was encouraged and renewed by her time away, by the letters George had faithfully written her, and by what appeared to be his longing for her return. She was, of course, sad to be separating again from Fred, but she knew it was for the best. Even so, she had always hated saying 'goodbye' and this one would be uncomfortable at best.

The two spent most of the evening recalling special moments of the past 10 weeks......walks by the seashore, sunset dinners at the finest resorts, luxury accommodations, and gathering treasures for Mary's nature journal. They laughed over their day in Tijuana and marveled at the awesome majesty of Yosemite. They talked of Mr. Branette's generous hospitality and lavish pampering, and of the purchase of Fred's orange grove three miles east of Ventura. They were able to chuckle now over how dreadfully altitude sick Mary had become while passing through Denver on the westbound trip.

"I'll never look at a glass of tomato juice the same way again!" she said laughingly.

This evening they were as relaxed with each other's conversation as they had always been through the years, and it was very good. The hours passed easily and comfortably.

"You have lavished me with flowers and gifts and everything a girl could ever want." Mary said quietly and then she smiled at him. "Thank you for everything," she said slightly raising her stemware. "This has been such a remarkable time, Fred, and I've been so very happy." She reached the very short distance across the settee and patted the back of his hand. He turned his hand over and held her hand in his.

"Will you remember, Mary that if you *ever* change your mind, there will *always* be a place in my heart and in my life for you?" Fred stated the facts with a deliberate calmness and clarity. He stressed specific words for emphasis and meaning. "Is there *any* doubt in your mind that I love you?" He continued without giving her a chance to answer. "Is there *any* doubt in your mind that I *love* little Fredericka and I would raise her as if she were *my own* child?"

Mary's heart was instantly gripped within her tightly laced bosom. A torrent of memories overwhelmed her, and glimpses and images of times past flashed like streaks of lightening before her. She took a very deep breath and closed her eyes. Silently, she exhaled, and then took in another slow breath. She realized she was squeezing his hand. She had to regain her composure before she could speak a word. She took another deep breath, looked into those incredible eyes, and began to speak. Softly she said, "No. There is no doubt in my mind whatsoever."

Sometime in the early morning hours, about 2:00 or 3:00 A.M., the train pulled into the station in Hays. Max helped Fred gather his belongings and disembark from the train. Mary chose not to dress and see them off, but watched from the privacy of her sleeping car. Her tears began to flow as soon as she saw Fred alight from the train onto the wooden plank platform. She watched as he tipped the trainman, generously she was sure, and then shake his hand. She knew he was thanking him for the excellent service while onboard, and instructing him one final time to watch over the two women who were continuing east. Max stood beside Fred holding his valise and hat. Once he handed them to his employer, the two men shook hands, and Max reboarded the train. Fred waved to his mother who was standing in the doorway; she had risen and dressed to see her son off. She blew him a kiss and waved heartily.

Mary could see Fred begin to scan the side of the coach for the window of her compartment. For a instant, she thought of quickly drawing the curtain, but she remained transfixed on his form in the dimly lit night. The train lurched forward with an enormous puff of smoke and a blast of the whistle. Just then, Fred spotted her and began running to catch up with her sweet face framed by the varnished oaken window of the departing coach. He waved and his pace quickened, as did the momentum of the train. Mary wiped her tears and smiled as broad a smile as she could muster and placed her open hand on the window. "Goodbye," she said softly, knowing that no one would hear her words, but he would know. He always knew.

She, of course, could not hear him shouting, "I love you! I'll always love you!" but she knew. She always knew.

Chapter 69

Mary resisted the strong urge to avoid breakfast the next morning out of courtesy for Aunt Emily. She was dreading the endless chatter that she knew her Aunt was prone to, especially when it was just the two of them. She arrived in the dining car looking as if she had not slept a wink all night, and, in fact, she hadn't. Aunt Emily was extraordinarily quiet and the two women passed the breakfast hour by picking at their meals, sipping tea and watching the countryside pass beyond them.

Over the course of the next couple of days, Mary spent large blocks of time alone; alone in her private compartment, alone in the library, and alone even in the public areas. She was, as always, polite to Aunt Emily but did not go out of her way to spend time with her. She mended dresses and blouses and wrote notes to many of her friends and cousins. She cried, and she napped. She was exhausted and wondered how she could feel so tired after such a lovely trip. Aunt Emily kept her eye on her, but gave her the room she needed; room to be alone.

On Friday, May 15, the last day on the train before reaching Rock Island, Aunt Emily located Mary in the library car writing a long letter to Mrs. Heron. Mary had met her earlier in the trip and the two instant friends intended to see each other again before leaving California. Unfortunately, their schedules had not meshed and plans were laid for meeting another time.

"I can only begin to tell you, Jennifer," Mary wrote, "what an important part you played. Just at the time when I needed a friend to talk to, our Lord sent you. I shall never forget our chat in the Tea Room, and was only sorry that my cousin interrupted our visit. I trust the remainder of your trip was enjoyable. I am enclosing my address in Hyattsville and will look forward to hearing from you and making arrangements to visit with you once we both return from our trips. There is a line that runs between Washington Union Station and Fredericksburg, and it should be easy for us to see each other on a fairly frequent basis."

Mary was rereading her note when Aunt Emily approached and asked if she could join her.

"Of course, I'd love to have you with me," and she was entirely serious. "I'm just finishing a letter to Jennifer Heron."

"Oh, she was that lovely young lady you met early on; the one you thought so highly of." Aunt Emily said as she gathered her skirts and sat across from Mary. "She was a Virginia lady, wasn't she? Wouldn't it be nice if you could see each other again? Do you think you will?"

"Yes, actually I'm sure we will. There was something special between us right from the start. I felt I'd known her all my life, and found her so easy to talk to."

Aunt Emily picked up a Harper's Weekly that was laying on the walnut end table and began leafing through it. "We all need those special people in our lives. To help us through the difficulties, I mean."

After a few minutes of silence, and delivery of a fresh pot of tea by the porter, Mary spoke guardedly. "You knew all along, didn't you, Aunt Emily?"

"Knew what, dear?" she said without looking up from her magazine.

"Knew that Fred intended to have me to stay with him in California."

It was unlike Aunt Emily to stammer, but this time she certainly did. It was almost funny.

"Umm...aaaa...well...uha...well, I...I suppose I *may* have *suspected* it." She was completely caught off guard and she knew she had not done a very good job of hiding the truth.

"It's alright, Aunt Emily, I'm not annoyed." Mary reassured her with a little smile.

"It's just that you were both *so terribly miserable*," Aunt Emily stressed as she looked at Mary and let the magazine flop into her lap. "It just absolutely breaks my heart to see any of my children upset, and you know I consider you one of my own. Here you and George were in such a dilemma; there just seemed no end in sight to your difficulties. As for Fred, why he's not been himself in years. He has *always* loved you, Mary dear, and you know that." Aunt Emily took a sip of tea and returned the pretty, delicate cup to its saucer. "I didn't know what would become of it, of course, but I thought some time together would do you and Fred both some good. It certainly would not do any *harm*, for heaven's sakes.

"Aunt Emily, I'm surprised at you!" Mary tried to sound stern but sounded much more light-hearted. "Need I remind you that I'm *married*...and what about the fact that Fred and I are first cousins?"

"Oh for heaven's sakes!" she retorted in shorts bursts of words. "Southerners marry their cousins all the time," she said swatting the air once with her left hand. She leaned close to Mary and added in a whisper, "Especially when there's *money* in the families!" She paused, then tacked on, "...and you *were* born in Louisiana."

At that, both women giggled and Mary refreshed their tea. From that time on there was no further discussion of the subject, but Mary and Aunt Emily both knew they had just shared a special conversation that would give them an even stronger bond throughout the years to come. Moreover, they both knew that Mary had come to the right decision, for the right reasons, all on her own.

In Hays, Fred was finding very little about which to laugh, and he was still questioning the wisdom of Mary's decision. He just didn't understand why she would chose to stay in what had thus far proven to be a difficult marriage. He would mull the details over and over in his mind, wondering if there was anything he could have said or done differently.

Immediately upon his return from California, he began making preparation for the sale of his land in Hays and his upcoming relocation to California. It would not be as he had wished; Mary would not be joining him. Her decision to remain with George had affected him deeply; more than he would ever let her know. He couldn't let her know how gravely disappointed he was, or how little hope he held for a happy future for Mr. and Mrs. George Smythe.

Chapter 70

Letter Forty-Seven

Rock Island Arsenal
May 16th, 1891

My dear Geo

We arrived here a little after 11 last eve. Hannah met us with carriage as Max was sick. We found a number of letters but I only had one from you. I think you must have spoiled me in the past by writing so often for I found myself quite disappointed that there was but one, and not a long one, for I've waited since the one at Salt Lake, but one is better than none. I wish you had told me about your plans if to come for me or not. Will have to wait till I reach Newark to write again.

Wish you might see how beautifully the Island is looking. Their home is lovely. Goes ahead of any of the other cousins' homes; is prettier than Ike's. He will be in Chicago on Wednesday. We pass him. Mark is still in command. This afternoon Hannah, the children, the officer's wife next door and I are all going to the circus this afternoon.

We leave here Monday; will be home (Newark) Wednesday.

I'm glad you have engaged Lulie for I don't think I could get along with house cleaning alone.

They write me the baby has another tooth and more coming. Poor little thing. Joseph Alfred is sick with his.

I do hope Mrs. Burnside will live. It would be a great loss. What would her dear little ones do?

This will be my last letter, dear, and now it is lunchtime. Have a letter at Newark please for me, that I may know your wishes.

Give much love to Natalie. I was much surprised and pleased to think Natalie was with you still. Yes, I should like to have heard Carrie Remsley.

No better news from Lydia. Josh is at home. Will have much to tell you.

Faithfully yours,
M

P.S.
You would enjoy yourself fishing here so much. They would make you so welcome too. Hannah goes into society a great deal; has been showing me her fine dresses this morning but nothing that money can buy or give takes the place of love. But that she has too for Mark is a devoted husband and father.

For the past 3 months I've had all money can give, but it is your love alone that gives me happiness.

Epilogue

To say that Mary and George "lived happily ever after" would be the ending found only in fairy tales. Mary returned to their home in Hyattsville refreshed and with a renewed commitment to her marriage, to George, and to the Lord. Her faith had moved from a once-a-week experience to a very personal relationship with Jesus Christ. She knew that she needed to trust Him in all things and place a high value on the eternal rather than momentary satisfaction. Both George and Mary, however, continued to be strong-willed people and clashes would erupt throughout their lives. Mary's faith sustained her, and she lived her life knowing she had made the right decision not to stay with Fred in California, in spite of periodic times of difficulty. She and George lived a financially comfortable life and she was able to afford the many treats she so much enjoyed.

Mary never wavered on her love for Fredericka, and, regardless of her own decision, was committed to raising her daughter with a great deal of devotion and attention. She never left her again for such an extended period. As the years passed, Fredericka would speak very little about her mother's trip to California.

In the spring of 1892, Mary gave birth to her second daughter, Florence Louise Smythe. The child died before her second birthday.

On December 30, 1893, Mary and George joyfully celebrated the birth of Eleanor Virginia Smythe. Fredericka, now four years old, and Eleanor, both beautiful little girls, would be the couple's only two children to survive to adulthood and the sisters would remain good friends throughout their lives.

Eventually, George and Mary were able to buy the home in

downtown Washington, D.C. that Mary referred to in these letters. It was the scene of many happy gatherings of family and friends.

George lived well up into his 80's and was a wonderful grandfather to my mother. She knew him and loved him very much, but could see where he "could be gruff" and had "rough edges" and "was probably hard to get along with." He died in 1942 and was buried in West Virginia where he had spent the last 20 years of his life.

Fred truly could not live without Mary. He became despondent when he realized all hope was lost of ever having Mary with him. He committed suicide in his orange grove in California in February 1892, less than a year after this trip took place. He was 32 years old. His body was returned to New Jersey for burial. He left a substantial sum of his wealth to his valet Max and the remainder of his large estate to his beloved Mary. Otherwise, his death was never discussed in Mary's presence.

Aunt Emily was carefully protected from the details surrounding her son's death and she never knew that he had taken his own life. She was told that he died of heart failure. She lived a healthy and feisty life, traveled frequently, and passed on peacefully in her sleep at age 74.

Mary's thirst for adventure was never completely satisfied, and she continued to travel extensively often throughout her lifetime. Letters and documents exist detailing her 1913 trip to Cuba, and in 1914, Mary had to be evacuated from Paris when World War I was declared. She expressed frustration at being unable to finish shopping while in Paris and having to leave in such a hurry.

Mary died in 1919 while on a trip to Cincinnati while visiting cousins. She was 61. At her request, her ashes were returned to New Jersey for burial. New Jersey had always been "home" and it was her desire to be laid to rest there. It was there, too, that Fred was buried.

The End

The Smythe home in Hyattsville, MD. Pictured are Natalie (left),
George holding Fredericka, Sophia (standing on porch)
and Mary (seated beside her mother Sophia).

Notes

1. Mary's husband George insisted that the two women would not travel alone and sent his valet to accompany them as far as Chicago. Once the women safely boarded the connecting train, he returns to George in Maryland. He is not mentioned otherwise.
2. "The Limited" refers to the name of the train. It is still "The Capital Limited" that runs between Washington, DC and Chicago, IL.
3. Julia and Edith Morrison; sisters; Mary's cousins
4. Johnstown, Pennsylvania. The scene of a devastating flood on May 31, 1889 when 2,209 people lost their lives and thousands more were injured in one of our nation's great disasters.
5. An old family friend, Major Gordon retired as a General. He lived far into his 90's and was known to Mary's descendants.
6. Natalie, Mary's sister-in-law, was an extremely large woman.
7. These original letters, written by Mary and "kept together" by her husband George, are the basis for this writing.
8. Joshua B. Remsley ("JBR") is another of Mary's many cousins, was suffering from severe depression.
9. Dr. and Mrs. Hart were family friends from Washington, DC. Mrs. Hart's sister was a Mrs. Gill from Kentucky.
10. Katherine (Kate) Remsley was a beloved cousin and dear friend.
11. Cousin Kate was a young widow. Her husband was tragically killed in a run-away carriage accident. They had been married only 8 days.
12. Cousin Joshua B. Remsley
13. Lydia Remsley was a dear friend, and cousin. George and Mary first met in Lydia's ice cream parlor in Cincinnati, OH.
14. The lovely Albany Hotel in Denver was built in 1885. Located within

the hotel were offices for Denver & Rio Grande Railroad, a drug-store and a café. The hotel was demolished in 1977.

[15] Maxwell Webster, Fred's personal valet was traveling with him.

[16] On the original letter, Mary has marked an "x" over the 2nd story hotel room showing exactly where they stayed.

[17] Mrs. Hilda Ungerford, a neighbor from Hyattsville, was originally from Ellsworth, Kansas. She often remarked that it was a tiny, dusty, 'one horse' town.

[18] Mrs. Olivia Anderson was another of Mary's friends who was active in the local garden club. Mary was working along with her to fund the new aviary, here referred to as "the cage."

[19] The two women had approached Mr. Albert Dunnton of the Evening Gazette Newspaper about funding their project. Mary anxiously awaited his response.

[20] Sherman, also known as "Lone Tree Pass" and later as "Evans Pass," is located 17 miles east of Laramie. At 8,262' above sea level, it is the highest point on the Union Pacific Railroad between the two coasts. The pyramid that Mary refers to is the Ames Monument built in 1882 as a memorial to the Ames Brothers for their services in the construction of the Union Pacific Railroad. As far as this author can determine, the monument has nothing to do with Sherman's march to the sea.

[21] Mr. Branette was an attorney and a prominent landowner in Cali-fornia. Fred was involved in land speculations and various business dealings with him, and they have become good friends.

[22] Mrs. Lucille Hamner was probably the most outwardly 'religious' of Mary's friends. At a recent going-away luncheon, Mrs. Hamner stood and pronounced a lengthy benediction over Mary, her family, her companions and every aspect of her upcoming trip.

[23] The six story Palace Hotel opened in 1875 as a hotel of "timeless elegance and unprecedented luxury." Its 1,200 guests enjoyed mar-vels such as the hotel's four hydraulic elevators known as "rising rooms" and suites equipped with call buttons so attendants could promptly fulfill their guest's every whim.

[24] California Senator George Hearst died February 28 in Washington,

DC. A six-car funeral train bearing his remains made its way across country, ending in San Francisco. Hearts' wife Phoebe, and son William Randolph, were on the train, along with many other U.S. senators and dignitaries.

[25] Mrs. Oster was an attractive young Washington widow who enjoyed the company of numerous older, and very wealthy, gentlemen. Although Mary found her to be extremely fascinating and admired her tenacity, most who knew her were critical of her somewhat brazen lifestyle.

[26] The 424' ferry, an engineering marvel of its time, carried Central Pacific railroad cars between Port Costa and Benicia. The giant ferryboat featured four sets of tracks capable of transporting two entire trains plus a switch engine.

[27] The Presidio has a long and historic presence in the San Francisco area including extensive Native American and military history. It is now part of the National Park Service Golden Gate National Recreation Area.

[28] Built in 1863, this cliff-side resort was frequented by San Francisco's most prominent families including the Hearst's and Stanford's. In 1881, self-made millionaire and philanthropist Adolph Sutro, once owner of the Comstock Silver Mine, purchased the property and built a railroad to bring guests to his seaside attraction. Three years after Mary's visit, the original structure was destroyed by fire. Since that time there have been a second and a third "Cliff House," which is now part of the National Park Service Golden Gate National Recreation Area.

[29] The Hotel Del Monte was a pioneer among luxury resorts and promoted itself as the "…most elegant seaside establishment in the world". Built in 1880, railroad tycoons built destinations and then the rails that brought the guests to them. The Del Monte encompassed tens of thousands of acres and preserved vast, unobstructed views of the spectacular countryside.

[30] Senator Sharon, owner of the Palace Hotel in San Francisco.

[31] James 1:5&6

[32] Another grand hotel, the Nadeau is said to have been the first four-

story building in Los Angeles. Letterhead stationery reads "Hotel Nadeau, Practically Fire-Proof, Rates: $2.50 to $4.00 per day. Bennett & Burns Bros. Proprietors"

[33] Mount San Antonio, the high point of the San Gabriel Mountains near Los Angeles, is also known as Mount Baldy.

[34] A multi-millionaire, Lucky Baldwin was known for his land holdings, pure luck in financial investments, and a harem of admiring women.

[35] "Freddie" is the nickname of baby Fredericka.

[36] Mary had been sending these letters to her husband at his place of employment: the main post office in Washington DC. His recent letter requested that she send her letters to their home address in Hyattsville, MD.

[37] One of the Lyton family cousins from Cincinnati, OH.

[38] Sect. P, mentioned here and in later letters, is unidentified.

[39] Lulie Coates was a beloved nanny and was with the Smith family for many, many years. She appears in later photographs holding a baby.

[40] Dr. Reynolds was an old family friend from Newark.

[41] Letterhead stationery touts that this resort includes "Fine Drives. Magnificent Scenery. The Greatest Orange Growing District in the World" and "The Popular Resort in Southern California for Health & Pleasure".

[42] "Mamma", meaning Mary's mother-in-law, George's mother.

[43] The world renowned Hotel Del Coronado, built in 1888, is a grand example of elegant Victorian architecture and is one of the world's largest wooden structures. Considered an oasis for society when the American West was still rugged and untamed, the original five-story, 400-room complex continues to provide an exceptional travel experience today. Two newer sections offer an additional 300 rooms. The Crown Room is regarded as one of the world's monumental architectural achievements. No nails or interior supports are in its 30' ceiling; it is held together solely with wooden pegs. In addition to countless presidents, international dignitaries, and celebrities, this author visited "The Del" in 1989. I sat in the grand lobby rereading

the words my great-grandmother penned there 100 years ago. I agree with Mary's assessment: "It is the finest hotel I ever saw."

[44] The Smith's wanted to buy a home in Washington, DC rather than where they were living in Hyattsville, MD.

[45] Dr. Bailey is the Pastor at the Presbyterian Church in Washington, DC where Mary and George are members.

[46] Psalm 73:2

[47] James 4:17

[48] Proverbs 3:5 & 6

[49] Ike, short for Isaiah, is Fred's oldest brother.

[50] Abe, is the middle of Fred's three brothers.

[51] "LaGripp" slang for the 'grip' or the flu.

[52] "As there is but one Santa Barbara in the World, so there is but one 'Arlington' in Southern California. The rooms are large and elegantly furnished, corridors broad, grounds ample…four and a half acres in extent…adorned with roses, shrubs, and palms. Here the weary may rest, the sick be healed, the active roam over mountain, hill and valley, or sail upon the ocean. Here is PEACE, HEALTH, COMFORT." This quote is taken from the Arlington Hotel stationery. With 90 rooms, the Arlington was the town's first luxury hotel, built in 1875 to welcome the new influx of tourists from the east. Mule-drawn trolley cars toted guests to the beach. The grand hotel burned to the ground in 1909 and is today the site of the Arlington Theatre.

[53] Mary marked the room in which she is staying by placing an "x" on the sketch of the hotel on the letterhead.

[54] Jay Gould (1836-1892) was a railroad financier. He was eventually a director of seventeen major railroads and the president of five. He purchased much Union Pacific stock and controlled that railroad until 1878. Upon his death in 1892, he left a fortune of an estimated $77 million to his six children.

[55] The author has numerous pages from this precious collection, given to her in 2000 by her cousins, the Reynolds Family of Tulsa, OK. They are as pristine today as they were 115 years ago when Mary and Fred gathered and pressed them. A note included with the

Reynolds' collection says, "These were gathered by my Grandmother on a very happy and special trip to California."

[56] "Josh Houses" served the Chinese community as central places of worship.

[57] As Mary never had sons, she is apparently referring to her husband, George, as her "big boy."

[58] Whist was a popular card game of the day.

[59] On April 25, 1891, President Benjamin Harrison visited San Francisco.

[60] Fred stood as Best Man at the marriage of George and Mary on January 27, 1887.The ceremony was held in Fred's parent's home in Newark, NJ; the home of Aunt Emily and Uncle Isaac where Mary had grown up.

[61] This paragraph is another indication of the difficulties that George and Mary had experienced in their marriage.

[62] Begun in the mid-1800 as a stage stop and primitive inn, Wawona is one of the oldest mountain resorts in California and is a National Historic Landmark. Lush meadows, rushing streams, and tranquility combine to make this an especially appealing location. The hotel is located four miles from the Yosemite's south entrance nestled between the Mariposa Grove of Big Trees and the Yosemite Valley.

[63] Sam, George's brother and Mary's brother-in-law, was a very large gentleman.

[64] Vernal Falls and Nevada Falls are a few miles apart and are two of the beautiful waterfalls within Yosemite National Park.

[65] The train was passing through remote parts of Nevada.

[66] Yet another reference to the difficulties Mary and George had been experiencing prior to her departure on this extended trip.

[67] Fort Douglas, established in October 1862, was named for the late Senator Stephen A. Douglas of IL. The Fort was listed on the National Register of Historic Places in 1970 and as a National Historic Landmark in 1975.

[68] The party is now traveling on the narrow-gage Denver and Rio Grande Railroad from Salt Lake City to Denver. The 10,200' Tennessee Pass

was a high point in rail route and revealed extraordinarily beautiful scenery. Today, the ski areas of Vail, Beaver Creek, and Copper Mountain are in this area.

[69] The 14,005' Mount of the Holy Cross is one of Colorado's most scenic and secluded peaks. Snow fills in the rocks and ravines to reveal a perfect cross the as large as the side of the mountain. The cross is best viewed from Notch Mountain.

[70] Mary describes Castle Gate, UT very well. The area was opened in 1888 when a coal seam was located and mining began. It will always be remembered for the tragic explosion on March 8, 1924; 171 men were killed. These rock formations was destroyed in the 1950's when the road was changed.

[71] The Black Canyon of the Gunnison afforded travelers awesome scenery. Rudyard Kipling, who rode through the canyon in 1889 is quoted, 'We entered a gorge, remote from the sun, where the rocks were two thousand feet sheer, and where a rock splintered river roared and howled ten feet below a track which seemed to have been built on the simple principle of dropping miscellaneous dirt into the river and pinning a few rails a-top. There was a glory and a wonder and a mystery about the mad ride, which I felt keenly…until I had to offer prayers for the safety of the train.'

[72] Mrs. President Benjamin Harrison

[73] Cousin Edith Morrison

[74] Aunt Elizabeth is the mother of Edith and Julie Morrison.

Printed in the United States
62744LVS00003B/331-357